1

'She'll be all right now,' Dr Amy Merrill said, replacing the little girl's arm beneath the blanket. She glanced at the attendant Nurse Chester, saw the blossoming relief in the timid young woman's face, and smiled, letting her professional manner slip for a moment. Everyone would be relieved now, she thought. The whole hospital staff had taken an interest in small Jane Gilmour, who had run away from that big mansion of a home on Pent's Hill to look for her lost mother. Poor little rich girl! The thought was uppermost in Amy's mind as she took up the chart and wrote upon it. She looked down at the flushed face of the sleeping child. It had been touch and go. The police had found the child asleep in the rain under a haystack, after a widespread search had been made of the town and the adjacent countryside.

Only a skilled person could tell the improvement in the laboured breathing that sounded. But the crisis was passed.

Amy felt great relief stirring through her as she left the children's ward. She had been worried about Jane ever since she first saw the child two days before. Pneumonia was a killer, and sight of the young face on the pillow had shaken her more than she cared to admit. For one heart-stopping moment Jane Gilmour had looked exactly like little Susan Merrill. Amy took a shuddering breath as she walked towards the waiting room to give the good news to Jane Gilmour's next of kin. There was no child named Susan Merrill. She had died with her father in a boating accident on the River Wendham one fine Sunday afternoon three years ago.

The pain that stabbed through Amy's heart was very real. Three years without a child and husband seemed like a lifetime, but Amy had not yet forgotten the anguish and heartbreak. At times she could still hear Susan's voice calling

DOCTOR'S DESTINY

Having lost her husband and daughter in a boating accident, Dr Amy Merrill lives with her aunt and uncle and works at the local hospital. Still struggling after three years to put the past behind her, she befriends a young patient, Jane, brought to the hospital with pneumonia. Jane, she discovers, has run away from her rich father's house to search for her lost mother. And when Amy meets the father, handsome Grady Gilmour, her life will never be the same again . . .

PHYLLIS MALLETT

DOCTOR'S DESTINY

Complete and Unabridged

LINFORD
Leicester

First published in Great Britain in 1968

First Linford Edition
published 2018

A catalogue record for this book is available
from the British Library.

ISBN 978–1–4448–3812–1

Published by
F. A. Thorpe (Publishing)
Anstey, Leicestershire

Set by Words & Graphics Ltd.
Anstey, Leicestershire
Printed and bound in Great Britain by
T. J. International Ltd., Padstow, Cornwall

This book is printed on acid-free paper

her, or Dave's happy tones ringing out in laughter. They had been a very happy family — until that Sunday afternoon three years ago.

Amy pushed open the door of the waiting room and entered. There was a tightness in her throat as she looked at Grady Gilmour. He attracted a great deal of interest in Barnbridge because his furniture factory was the first of its kind in the Suffolk county town, and heralded the approach of a new era. There had long been talk that Barnbridge would become an overspill town for London, and now the first of the factories was in operation and another was in the process of being built.

Gilmour was not an old man, as she had at first supposed, and Amy was a little surprised to see that he was no more than a few years older than her thirty-one. She had seen him from a distance more than once, and of course his picture had been in the local paper many times. He stood up now, staring into her face that training and schooling had made expressionless at times like this. She nodded, permitting a smile to cross her features.

'Good news, Mr Gilmour,' she said quietly. 'Jane is over the crisis. She's going to be all right.'

His sigh echoed through the little room, his shoulders rising and falling. He had blue eyes, and they seemed overbright as he stared at her. Then he nodded, a smile coming to his rugged face.

'Thank you, Doctor,' he said huskily. 'Thank God that's over. It's been like a nightmare.'

'It may not be over,' Amy said slowly, prompted by something that welled up from deep inside.

'What do you mean?' He was anxious again. 'Complications?'

'Of a sort, I shouldn't wonder, but not medical complications. This part of it is none of my business, but Jane ran away from home. That's what started all this. What if she should try the same thing again, when she's well?'

'I've already thought of that.' He

nodded slowly, thinning his lips. His eyes were dark circled. He hadn't left the waiting room for more than an hour at a time since Jane had been admitted. 'I'm worried about it. I don't know what got into her this time. She's always been a good, well-adjusted child. There was no hint of this before it happened.'

'I heard that she ran away to look for her mother.'

Grady Gilmour stared at her for a moment, his eyes studying her intent face. He saw concern in her brown eyes, and he nodded slowly.

'I know what you're thinking,' he said. 'I'm a businessman, and I haven't got any time for my daughter.'

'You said that,' Amy told him.

'And it's true. Jane misses her mother, and I can't replace a mother in that child's heart. I've done what I can. I've given her everything she could possibly need in this life; toys, money, clothes, books. You name it and I bought it. But I can't give her a mother's love. I've engaged the best nurses, governesses and companions, but to no avail. Jane wants her mother back, and that's an impossibility.'

There was silence that seemed to hang heavily while they stared at one another. Grady Gilmour took a long, bitter breath. He shook his head and pulled a face as his thoughts ran over his past.

'Her mother left me for another man,' he said tensely. 'I claimed Jane because her mother didn't want her. The divorce came through and that was the end of everything. I lost myself in business, and I made a fortune because of it. That was the only good thing Marion did for me. She made me angry enough to devote all my energies to business. But poor Jane had nothing to turn to.' He sighed angrily. 'Perhaps I did the wrong thing by taking her away from her mother, but a loving father is better than a don't-care mother, isn't that right?'

'I'm sure it is, but a child wouldn't

think so.' Amy studied him, head on one side. 'We'll take good care of Jane while she is with us, but you'd better make some arrangements for later.'

'Have you got any suggestions?' He was desperate now. 'I don't care what it costs. Just so long as nothing happens to Jane. She's all I've got left in this world.'

It was a cry from his heart, and Amy was touched. She smiled thinly. Jane's mother hadn't wanted her child, had gone off and left her. There seemed to be no justice in the world. Another woman loved her family passionately, more than life itself, and she lost them, was condemned to a life of emptiness because of a cruel stroke of fate.

'I'll do what I can.' Amy could say no more than that. 'Jane will be with us for a week or two, given normal progress. It's a breathing space.'

'I'm eternally grateful to you,' he said, coming nearer. His eyes bored into her. 'You seem to have a nice way with you, Doctor. Can I hire you to take care of Jane for me?'

'I'm here to help everyone who needs it,' Amy said. 'It wouldn't be right to deprive all the others, would it?'

'You're right, but I'm desperate about this. I thought I had an answer to everything, but these past two days have shown me just how little I can accomplish. For the first time in a good many years I've had the time to think straight. I thought I was doing the right thing by burying myself in business, making money.' There was a contemptuous note in his tones that Amy did not miss. 'But all the time I've been ignoring the most precious thing — Jane. Do you think it's gone too far? Have I made a mistake that can't be rectified?'

'I don't think so. A child's mind is resilient. Jane might forget her troubles if she had enough love and understanding from her remaining parent.'

'I know what you mean,' he said fervently. 'If there is a chance of putting her mind right then I'll take it. The business can go hang now.'

Amy nodded, smiling faintly. It was good to see a man who put his child's well-being first. But that was the way of it in this world, she told herself bitterly. One didn't appreciate the gold at one's feet until something happened to remove it. A husband and a daughter had been her blessings, and she had lost them. She had appreciated them at the time, but only after they had been lost did she really understand the true purpose in life.

Grady Gilmour took her hands impulsively. He gripped them tightly, and it was the first time that a man had touched Amy since her husband died. She stiffened, but already he was releasing her and moving away, impatient after his long hours of vigil, restless from the relief that swamped through him.

'I'll ring first thing in the morning,' he said. 'I'll be along to see her tomorrow afternoon.'

'You can visit the children's ward at

any time during the day,' Amy said mechanically.

'Thank you. Goodnight.'

Amy drew a long breath. He had suffered every torment in the past few days, waiting and hoping that his daughter would live. Now he knew the danger had passed and he would start living again, probably forgetting all the prayers he had offered up during his long vigil. By the time his daughter was fit to be discharged he would have let his mind sink back into its complacent rut and all would have been forgotten.

She went back to the ward and looked at the child. It was obvious that Jane Gilmour was over the worst of it. Nurse Chester hovered close by, and Amy nodded encouragingly as she turned and departed. A few days would see a great change in the child's condition.

Amy glanced at her watch as she pushed through the swing doors. She was late going off duty this evening, but she had never been one to work by the clock. The job of healing and nursing was continuous, and a nurse or doctor who worried about time was not suited to hospital work. She felt tired, her feet aching as she walked wearily to her small office. She had promised Aunt Marjorie to be home early, and already it was nearly ten. She smiled to herself. Aunt Marjorie, married to a general practitioner for thirty years, knew the details of life among the medical people. A doctor was at everyone's beck and call.

She sighed her exasperation when she finally left the hospital and stared around the car park. She had left her car at home that afternoon, accepting a lift by her uncle, and now she would have to take a bus. She felt a spot of rain on her face as she left the hospital grounds and walked towards a bus stop. The local service was intermittent, and she checked her watch, realising that she could walk the two miles home before a bus arrived. Rain was beginning to fall quite heavily, and she smiled thinly as she turned up the collar of her coat and started walking.

Her mind was filled with disturbing thoughts, and only a part of it concentrated upon the mechanical action of walking. She couldn't get the sight of little Jane Gilmour out of her brain. There had been something pathetic in the youngster; in the reason for the child's escapade. Because her heart was filled with grief for her own dead child, she felt a strand of close sympathy that arose to swamp the dead feelings inside. What could she do to help Jane Gilmour? She pictured the face of the child's father. He had been desperate back there in the waiting room. But all his money couldn't help him find a solution. Human emotions and material things did not mix. One could not supplant the other. Money helped in making a life comfortable, but it could not take the place of a person. Her heart ached for the little girl in the narrow hospital bed. At seven years Jane Gilmour should have been getting her happiest impressions of family life, a grounding in balanced living to prepare her for her own adult years. But the child was as empty and unhappy as the doctor who cared for her.

The rain began to drum upon the pavements, and Amy stepped into a shop doorway to await the passing of its heavy attack. She must have been preoccupied to leave her car at home, she thought. But Uncle Ronald had said he would be passing the hospital at six-thirty, and he would have picked her up had she been ready to go home. She smiled to herself. It was past ten now. Not even a husband would have waited all that time!

When she went on she wondered what she could do to help Grady Gilmour. It would be no use making snap decisions. A girl's life was on the scales. It would depend upon the way Jane Gilmour responded to treatment. The hospital could cure her illness, but the state of her mind was another matter. A girl who ran away from home to look for her mother showed a desperate need for love, understanding and assurance, which she would not get from her father, no matter the good intentions of Grady Gilmour. Perhaps irreparable harm had already been done to Jane's outlook.

She halted at the kerb, and saw a car approaching fast, its lights glaring off the wet road. She waited for it to pass, hunching her shoulders against the slashing rain, and as the car went by she started across the road. But there was a squeal of rubber on wet tarmac, and the brake lights of the car glowed redly. She stared at the vehicle as it stopped, wondering if it belonged to someone who knew her. A head was stuck out of the side window.

'Doctor, can I give you a lift?'

Amy turned towards the car, unable to recognise the voice, but as she drew nearer she saw Grady Gilmour's face peering at her.

'Can I give you a lift?' he repeated.

'If you're going along Queen Street

then I should be grateful,' she replied.

'That's a long walk,' he replied. 'Come and jump in.'

She walked around the car and he leaned sideways and opened the door for her. Amy got in beside him, sighing her relief. She slammed the door and he drove swiftly along the street.

'Haven't you got a car?' he demanded.

'Yes, but my uncle gave me a lift this afternoon, and I would have met him in time to drive home if I hadn't stayed on at the hospital.'

'And you stayed on because of Jane?'

'Partly. I was worried about her.'

'You were worried about her?' he echoed.

'Of course!' Amy glanced at his profile, and saw surprise in his handsome features. 'Do you think we doctors are inhuman, that our patients are just so many sick bodies that have to be healed? We are human, you know.'

'My thoughts were not quite on that line,' he replied, 'but you aren't far from the mark. What I was getting at is the number of people who come under your care in a year. If you worry about them all then you must be suffering with ulcers. I think I am, and I'm only a businessman.'

Amy smiled. She could hear the relief in his tones as he spoke, and knew what he must be feeling inside. His daughter was past the crisis in her illness, and his world was returning to normal.

'You know,' he said, glancing at her. 'I always feel guilty when I come into contact with your kind of people. You're so damned important to our community. You work long hours, and it's more than a job to you. It's a way of life. You're underpaid and overworked, and there's me earning thousands each year, and what do I contribute to society?'

'We can't do without furniture,' Amy said with a laugh.

'You know what I'm getting at,' he retorted. 'This isn't something that's come to mind just because my daughter is in your care. I've often thought like that. Perhaps I'd do well to try and ease my conscience by donating a couple of

16

beds, or something.'

'If you feel like that then get in touch with the hospital secretary,' Amy told him. 'But you don't owe us anything for taking care of Jane.'

'I'm desperately worried about Jane,' he went on. 'What can I do to help her? She must be the loneliest little girl in the world. I'm out of touch with her. I realize that now. I'd give anything to have that easy father-daughter relationship that one reads about.'

'Money can't buy a child's love.' Amy tightened her lips against the emotion that swelled inside her like an encompassing wave. She had almost forgotten what it was like to feel the arms of a small child clinging around her neck, to hear whispered words of love and confidence. She had lost all that, and she had thought that by returning to hospital life and devoting herself to other children she would do something towards filling the dead, barren spaces in her heart. But it was not so. The emptiness remained. Nothing could ever replace the loss of a daughter.

'Queen Street,' Grady Gilmour said. 'Where do you live?'

'At the doctor's house. The big one on the corner opposite the church.'

'Is the doctor your father?' he demanded.

'My uncle. My parents are dead. My aunt brought me up.'

'So you're local, one of the natives.'

'Yes. You're not, are you?'

'No. I came from London. The worst day's work I ever did. Still, I'm better off without Marion. The trouble with a broken home is the child that's left.' He brought the car to a halt in front of the four-storey house where Amy lived. 'There you are. If I'd known you were about to leave the hospital I would have waited for you.'

'You're very kind, Mr Gilmour.'

'My pleasure. Perhaps I shall see you at the hospital. How long will Jane have to stay in there?'

'It's early days yet,' Amy told him, smiling. 'Ask me again in a week.'

She opened the door and slipped out into the wet night. She bent low to peer in at him, and Gilmour was smiling.

'Goodnight, and thank you,' she called.

'Goodnight, Doctor,' he replied.

Amy went into the big house and stripped off her wet coat. Her uncle's study door opened, and Ronald Davis peered out at her. He was tall, thin, with a slightly stooped figure. His brown eyes regarded her for a moment.

'Why didn't you ring me, Amy?' he demanded. 'I would have come for you. You didn't get that wet coming home by bus, did you?'

'No, Uncle,' she replied, smiling. 'I walked part of the way, and then got a lift.'

'A lift,' he echoed.

'Father of one of my patients,' she said with a smile. 'Where's Aunt?'

'In the sitting room. Tony is with her.'

'Oh.' Amy's tones were non-committal, and her uncle smiled.

'He's a good man, and he's been waiting all evening to see you. It's disgraceful, the way you can't make definite plans because of that hospital. You should come into general practice, my girl.'

'You're tied as much as I,' Amy told him, smiling. 'I'll get dried out before I present myself to Aunt and Tony. But if I know Tony he wouldn't care how I looked.'

'His is a lost cause, I think,' her uncle said. 'Excuse me, Amy, I'm in the middle of a lot of urgent work.'

He withdrew and closed the door of his study. Amy sighed and went into the kitchen to dry off, then she went up to her room to change. She put on a green dress and flat-heeled shoes, did what she could to her hair, and then went down to the sitting room. She paused outside the door and listened to the voices coming from within, and a sigh escaped her as she opened the door and mentally steeled herself to face Tony Walker. It wasn't that he was not personable, she thought. But she knew his real motives in calling at her aunt's house. Tony Walker was in love, and the object of his feelings was still grieving a lost husband and daughter.

Tony Walker got to his feet when he saw Amy, and she stared into his good-looking face. At twenty-five he had made a fine start to his life in his father's law business. In a town such as Barnbridge, a solicitor commanded a deal of respect.

'Hello, Amy,' he greeted. 'I thought you were staying on all night. Do you have to work such long hours?' His blue eyes were filled with genuine concern, and Amy smiled.

'Hello, Tony. The sick are ill twenty-four hours a day, you know.' She crossed to the table where he and her aunt were sitting, and bent to kiss Aunt Marjorie's wrinkled forehead.

'Tired, dear?' Marjorie Davis demanded, her pale eyes studying Amy's weary face. 'How is your special patient?'

'Jane Gilmour?' Amy moved around the table and sat down by the fire. 'She's over the worst of it.'

'Good. Perhaps you'll stop your

worrying now and relax.' Aunt Marjorie got to her feet. 'I'll get you something to eat. I'll bet you didn't think of getting something at the hospital, did you?'

'I didn't.' Amy smiled. 'Sit down, Aunt. Don't bother now. I'll have some supper later.'

'I insist,' her aunt said, moving to the door. She was a small woman, with a kindly face and a deep reservoir of concern for her niece. 'Will you have something, Tony?'

'Just a cup of coffee please, Aunt,' he said.

Marjorie Davis departed quickly, and Tony came to the opposite side of the fire, sinking into an easy chair and staring into Amy's taut face.

'You're working much too hard,' he said at length. 'Amy, you're a source of worry to me, your aunt and your uncle.'

'Perhaps I should have gone in for law practice,' she said with a smile. 'You seem to get plenty of free time.'

'Why can't you be serious when I talk to you?' he demanded. There was an urgency in his tones that Amy recognised. He was in love with her, she knew, and yet she could not drive him away by revealing her true thoughts on that subject. Her aunt thought that three years of mourning were enough for a still-young woman. But thirty years would not remove the agony and grief. A mother had lost her child in a boating accident, along with the husband she had loved so dearly. Three years could not wipe out all the memories! People who had not suffered such a blow could not understand that.

'I'm the most serious woman in the world,' she replied, smiling.

'No you're not,' he complained. 'You know I want to talk to you about the future, but each time I come close to broaching the subject you put up a wall in your mind.'

'I hadn't noticed. I don't do it deliberately, Tony. I think you're a nice man, and you're a dear friend. You've helped me considerably since the tragedy.'

'You said you wouldn't talk about that any more.' He sighed and got to his feet. 'I hate to see you falling to pieces inside, Amy. You deserve a good break. You need to forget all that's happened. We have only one life, and it's our duty to make it as pleasant as we can. I think I can help you. I love you, and you know it. I've told you before, although not in so many words. Will you consider me, Amy?'

'I've told you before that my mind hasn't recovered from the tragedy,' she replied in a low voice. 'I have no thoughts of love or anything resembling it in my mind. Those seeds need fruitful ground, and inside I'm just like a desert. You're wasting your time, Tony, and that's a pity. I don't want our friendship to suffer because of this arising situation, so you'd better drop the subject if you can. I don't blame you for getting impatient, but you don't know how I feel.'

'I think I do,' he said slowly. He got to his feet with a sigh. 'Perhaps I am impatient, but one of these days you're going to suddenly fling off this cloak of mourning, and I'm afraid that I shan't be the first man you set your eyes on.'

'You're talking as if there's a string of fellows tied to my belt,' Amy told him, smiling.

'I know.' He shook his head, smiling ruefully. 'I just want to help you, Amy. I wish you'd let me.'

'Not right now,' she replied softly.

'All right. I shan't mention the subject again. I dropped by this evening to see if you will be free on Sunday. A party of us are going on the cabin cruiser. The summer is past, and there won't be many more nice days to take the boat out.'

'No thanks.' Amy's face was bleak, her mind filled with the sight of a summer afternoon on the river. 'You know I'm afraid of the water now. I wouldn't go on a boat to save my life.'

'You've got to start facing up to life again, Amy,' he said desperately. 'Three years have passed. Your mind has become conditioned to the situation. Make an effort to push forward again and it will get easier as you go along.'

'Thanks for the advice,' she said. 'I know exactly what's wrong with my mind, and what you say makes sense. But it's easier to give advice than to take it, and that's the whole trouble.'

'I feel so helpless,' he said, pacing the floor, his eyes on her face. 'I want to do so much to help you, Amy, but there is no way through for me. I just don't know what to try next.'

'Why not give up trying?' she countered. 'I'll snap out of it in my own good time.' As she spoke there appeared a picture of Grady Gilmour in her mind, and her heart seemed to miss a beat. She thought of the child, poor little Jane Gilmour, and emotion stabbed through her like a hot knife. The only way she could help herself was by helping others. That much she had learned in three dead years. But how could she help the Gilmours?

'I can see that you're slipping away

from me,' Tony Walker said with a sigh. 'I'll say goodnight now.'

'But your coffee,' Amy declared.

'I'll call into the kitchen on my way out.' He smiled at her. 'Goodnight, Amy. I'll see you again. Try not to work so hard. You're not the only doctor at the hospital.'

He left the room, and Amy relished the silence. She could hear the rain beating against the window, and the warmth of the fire was cosy. She hunched forward, extending her hands to the blaze. Her thoughts revolved upon the past, as they had done ever since the tragedy. It was as if the grim incident had frozen everything inside her, pinned her to that tragic time. Her memory, instead of being the wonderful comfort that it should be, had turned against her, acting like a goad with each impression and thought that reminded her of the old days, before the accident. And it would always be like that, she thought . . .

2

After a restless night Amy was relieved to get into her car and drive to the hospital. She was happiest when deep in work, and leisure time had no meaning for her. She parked in the grounds of the hospital and hurried into her office, divesting herself of her coat and putting on her white overall. Routine was an invaluable thing, and she followed it strictly. The morning round of the patients under her care was always a rewarding business, she found, and most of them were children. She found solace in taking care of children, and more than once she had caught herself calling some sick child by the name of her daughter who had died. She knew better than most the need in her that had to find satiation.

She had a way with children. She had always known that, but the fact had been brought home to her completely after the tragedy. She could always get some sick child to take medicine without trouble where the nurses had to wage war. She was a familiar sight, letting the children play with the stethoscope, giving them latitude as they became better. There was no end to her patience, nothing that seemed too much trouble, and if she made a promise then it was rigidly kept. She handled the worried parents, feeling for them in their anxiety, trying to soothe their fears, giving them hope, and she herself was hopeless. Each sick child was a challenge to the Fates that had destroyed the very meaning of her own life, and each victory a sweet experience to be savoured when the pangs of grief struck hard, as they did at times when her mind was relaxed and temporarily free of duty.

She found more improvement in Jane Gilmour's condition, and was heartened as she conversed with Sister Lockwood, in charge of the children's ward. When she went back to her office to handle the appointments, she was very near to happiness — not the heart swelling emotion of earlier years, but a satisfied feeling that she was on the winning side. The morning passed all too quickly, as usual, and she took lunch and resumed her work. During the afternoon there was a tap at the door of the office, and she put down her pen and got to her feet.

The door opened as she moved towards it, and Grady Gilmour peered in, smiling when he saw her. Amy paused and stared at him.

'Good afternoon, Doctor,' he said, smiling. 'I just had to tell you how relieved I am with Jane. She's beginning to take notice. She actually smiled at me.'

'Come in, Mr Gilmour,' Amy said, and moved back around her desk.

He closed the door and sat down in the seat beside the desk, leaning back and regarding her closely. He was quite at home in the little office, Amy could see, and this afternoon he had recovered from the strain which had assailed him during the past few days.

'I must have an attack of conscience,' he said, grinning, 'and a bad one at that. I'd like to show my appreciation for what's been done for my daughter. I didn't realize until I almost lost her just how much she means to me. How do I contact this hospital secretary you spoke of last night?'

'Do you wish to see him now?' Amy reached out for the telephone.

'Please. I'll make a donation to the hospital.'

Amy contacted the secretary's office, watched by Grady Gilmour, and she could feel a pang of mental discomfort assailing her as she felt the intensity of his gaze. His blue eyes were the palest she had ever seen, and they seemed to probe deeply into her soul.

'Hello,' she called, 'this is Amy Merrill. Is Mr Franklyn available?'

'Just a moment,' came the reply. 'I'm putting you through.'

'This is John Franklyn,' a husky voice cut in. 'Hello, Amy, what can I do for you?'

'I have a Mr Gilmour in my office,' she said, raising her eyes to meet Gilmour's gaze. 'He has some business to discuss which seems to come within your province. May I bring him along to see you?'

'Give me ten minutes,' Franklyn said. 'I've Matron with me at the moment, and it's important. That new wing for the Chest Clinic, you know.'

'Nothing must interrupt that,' Amy said with a smile. 'I'll be along presently.'

She hung up the receiver, trying to avoid Gilmour's eyes but failing to tear her gaze away. She leaned forward, her elbows on the desk and clasping her hands.

'He's busy at the moment, but if you won't mind waiting ten minutes I'll take you along to his office.'

'I'm free for the afternoon,' he replied quickly. 'I've decided to take some time for myself. This business game is too damned demanding. I pay a good staff to handle the work, and still keep the reins in my hands. Well they can start earning their salaries now. This business with my daughter has opened my eyes. Isn't it easy how one can blind oneself? I was pushing along in the same old way, thinking that everything was as usual, and my daughter was approaching a climax in her young life. It isn't right for a child of her age to be subjected to that kind of trouble. What a fool I've been! You're not married, are you, Doctor?'

'No.' Amy replied shortly, glancing down at her bare fingers. She had removed her wedding ring when she returned to hospital work.

'Then you don't understand what it means when something happens to your own child. It's different. A runaway wife is something a man can get over, but a child, one's own flesh and blood!'

The blue eyes in his strong, reliable

face seemed to glow, and Amy felt a tremor of emotion. It was good to see passion in a man, the emotions that stemmed from father-instinct. Her heart beat a trifle faster as she studied him. He glanced around the office, relaxed in his seat, his big hands clasped before him, his elbows resting on the arms of the chair.

'Is there anything I can bring in for Jane?' he demanded. 'I asked her but she shook her head. I suppose she's still too ill to know yet. Have you got any suggestions?'

'Leave her for a few days,' Amy advised. 'When she's able to sit up and take notice we'll try and get through to her.'

'She wouldn't talk to me,' he went on. 'There was an expression in her eyes that cut through me. It's as if she blames me for her mother's absence. If only she knew what I went through trying to keep Marion with us; not for my sake but for Jane's.'

'Children don't understand, Mr Gilmour,

but when she grows up Jane will understand, and she'll appreciate everything.'

'Do you think so?' His eyes lit up with hope. 'I can't imagine Jane grown up. I'll bet she'll be a pretty girl.' He shook his head as he smiled reflectively. 'We'll have some fun when she is old enough to start going around. Time will soon pass. She'll forget about her mother. Other things will take Marion's place.'

Amy smiled as she got to her feet. She walked around the desk to the door, and Gilmour got to his feet and moved ahead of her. He was tall and broad-shouldered, and she felt dwarfed as she passed him to leave the office. They walked together along the corridors, and Amy led him across a wide quadrangle to the administration block. When she paused outside John Franklyn's office Gilmour stared at her.

'I hope I shall see you again, Doctor,' he said.

'I shall be here every day,' Amy responded, 'and I'm always happy to talk to the parents of my patients.'

'Well I hope we shan't find Jane too much of a problem when she gets better. I don't want her running off again.'

Amy tapped at the door, heard John Franklyn's husky invitation to enter, and opened it. She escorted Grady Gilmour in and introduced the two men, leaving quickly. As she made her way back to her own office she felt strangely excited. Her world had so narrowed down in the past three years that even the slightest change in routine was something to look forward to.

She went back to the wards to check upon the seriously ill patients. The nurses were busy with their routine. Tea trolleys were in the wards. The younger patients were being fed. Amy stopped by Jane Gilmour's bed, automatically taking the girl's pulse. Blue eyes stared up at her, and she smiled encouragingly.

'Hello, Jane,' she said softly. 'How are you feeling now?'

The child did not answer, but regarded her seriously with fever-bright eyes. Amy was pleased with the patient's condition, and checked the chart. She heard a crash of cutlery and crockery, and looked up quickly. There was a sudden spate of upraised voices in the corridor, and then silence. Amy walked out of the ward, and as she expected, Nurse Halfnight was bending over a dropped tray and a spread of smashed plates and mugs. Sister Lockwood was scolding, but everyone knew it was useless. Nurse Halfnight was an awkward type, and accidents occurred regularly with her.

Sister Lockwood looked up and caught Amy's glance, raising her eyes ceilingwards in mock resignation. Nurse Chester appeared and helped clean up the mess. Order was quickly restored, and Amy went on her way. Crisis followed crisis in a hospital, and one became accustomed to the incessant challenges.

She met James Danby in a corridor, and paused to talk to the surgeon, who had emerged from a private room.

Danby was a man in his early forties, heavily built without being fat, and a genial man with surprisingly gentle hands for his bulk. He was a first-class surgeon and a good man for the staff. Danby had a soft spot for Amy. He had known her in the old days, before she had qualified or married, and they were good friends.

'You're looking pleased with yourself,' he commented.

'Me?' Amy stared at him in surprise. 'What are you talking about, James?'

'Have I said something wrong?' he demanded. 'I just made a remark, that's all. I'm sorry if you haven't got anything to be pleased about, and if you haven't then you should make a point of finding something every day to get happy over. You look twice as beautiful with a smile on your face.'

'Are you telling me that I was walking along this corridor with a silly smile on my face?' Amy demanded. They were old enough friends to be able to chaff each other.

'I wouldn't go so far as to say that,' he replied, grinning. 'But you were definitely pleased about something.'

'One of my patients, I expect. Little Jane Gilmour is showing improvement.'

'I know her father. He's been dreadfully worried about her. He's a nice chap. I was talking to him a few minutes ago, as a matter of fact. He asked me all kinds of questions about you. Wanted to know if you were good enough to take care of his daughter, no doubt.'

'Did he actually say that?' A sudden coldness gripped Amy as she waited for his reply.

'Of course not. He was singing your praises really, saying what a fine doctor you were. I had no idea you knew him. He's a guest of ours quite frequently. Coming around this evening. Would you like to come? Penny was saying only yesterday that you should get out more. I had intended asking you earlier today, but I clean forgot. I know it's at short notice, but please do come. You need a break sometimes, and Penny often says that she's sure she's done something to offend you. Once upon a time we saw quite a lot of you, but lately you've been hiding.'

Amy smiled. James Danby was quite a charmer. In the old days they had often gone out as a foursome, before Susan came along, she thought, and tried to stifle that thread before it got hold of her. She took a long breath.

'I'm going to surprise you, James,' she said with a smile. 'I accept your kind invitation. What time shall I show my pretty face?'

'Any time you wish. You're one of the privileged few. Our door is never shut to you, Amy.'

She glanced at her watch. 'Say seven-thirty?' she asked.

'That'll be fine. I shall look forward to seeing you. If you don't turn up then don't you dare show your face in my operating theatre again.'

'We shall have a busy day of it tomorrow,' Amy remarked. 'I have five children for you.'

'I've seen the list. Now I must hurry, or I shan't be at home to greet you when you arrive. I'll give Penny a ring shortly and tell her the good news.'

'About me?' Amy smiled. 'I've never been in such demand before in my whole life.'

'Your life hasn't really started yet,' he responded, and hurried away as he saw the hurt that came into her dark eyes.

Amy went on back to her office, relieved now the day's work was over. After a string of late nights she felt no compunction at leaving on time this evening, and she was strangely excited as she took off her overall and put on her coat. She walked into the children's ward before leaving, as was her habit, and satisfied that everything was in order she took her leave. Her steps quickened unusually as she went into the car park, and she didn't hear the voice that called to her twice before a hand reached out and touched her arm. She turned quickly, startled out of her

41

racing thoughts, and found John Franklyn staring at her.

'Well I never!' he declared. 'You must be getting deaf, Amy. I called you twice and you took no notice.' His brown eyes were keen as they took in her expression and animated eyes. 'Is anything wrong?'

'Certainly not! Should there be?' She smiled as she watched him. 'What can I do for you, John?'

'I just wanted to tell you about Gilmour's visit this afternoon. He wrote us out a cheque for two thousand pounds.'

'Conscience money,' Amy said. 'And he's greatly relieved that his daughter is all right.'

'I don't care what kind of money it is,' Franklyn replied, walking at her side as they crossed the park. 'I wish more of our rich patients would feel like that. He's an extremely generous man. How is his daughter, by the way?'

'She's progressing. But he has several problems to face when she is well enough to return home.'

'I wouldn't call that big showplace on Pent's Hill a home.'

'Perhaps that's the trouble,' Amy retorted. She paused by her car. 'I've promised to try and help with the girl, but I would say the solution lay in his own hands.'

'Yes. You'd better stick to medicine and leave the human side of it to the Almoner. Anyway, I'm glad he's been so generous. We can get on with our plans now.'

Amy smiled as she shook her head. She watched him walk along to his car, his thoughts on his problems. Everyone had problems, she told herself as she climbed into her car, but she was not concerned with her own for once as she drove home.

Aunt Marjorie was surprised when Amy informed her of her plans for the evening, but she covered her feelings quite well as she agreed that it would make a change. The older woman studied the young face, and was relieved at what she saw. After three years of unremitting grief the tension was about to lift. It happened quite suddenly, she knew, and was happy for her niece.

Amy dressed carefully, and spent a long time on her light brown hair. When she was ready to leave she wondered why she was taking all the trouble. James and Penny Danby were old friends, and she smiled at her reflection in the mirror. Was she hoping to impress Grady Gilmour? She said the name aloud as it came into her mind, and decided that it had quite an interesting ring about it. Then she snapped herself out of the thought and went down to bid goodbye to her aunt. She drove slowly to the Danby house, set in a quite pastoral area on the edge of town, and parked the small red Mini behind the big Bentley that took up most of the space near the gate. She surveyed the Bentley as she climbed out of her car and locked the door. King-sized, she thought, and it suited

Grady Gilmour. It was the car in which he had taken her home, and she stifled the half-longing that seeped up from some dark recess of her mind.

What was happening to her emotions? She wondered about it as she entered the gateway and walked along the leaf-strewn path to the house. The door opened before she got there, and Penny Danby stood beaming at her.

'Amy,' the woman exclaimed, her dark eyes alight with pure joy. 'I just couldn't believe it when James rang and said you had agreed to come for the evening. The times I've told him to ask you, and the times you've given him the same negative answer.'

'I'm sorry, Penny,' Amy responded. 'I must get out a bit more than I have been doing. I have neglected the social round lately, haven't I?'

'Never mind, dear. There's time for you to make up for lost time.'

'I was always taught that lost time cannot be regained,' Amy quoted, stepping across the threshold. She slipped out of her coat and Penny Danby took it into the cloakroom. Amy looked at her reflection in the hallstand mirror, and was pleased with what she saw, and received a slight shock. There was unaccustomed colour in her cheeks, and her eyes were brighter than she could ever remember seeing them.

'Come along,' Penny said, beaming, her blue eyes filled with glee. 'I've got someone here who wants to see you.'

'Really? I didn't know I had any friends in Barnbridge.'

'Amy!' There was mock severity in the tones.

They entered the large sitting room, and Grady Gilmour stood up and faced them as they crossed the rugs towards him.

'I know you two have met,' Penny said, smiling. 'But in case you came up against the formal Doctor Merrill, Grady, I'll make a social introduction here and now. Grady, this is Amy.'

'How do you do, Amy,' he said in mock solemn tones, and his blue eyes were sparkling in the firelight that flickered through the room.

'I'm pleased to meet you, Grady,' Amy replied with fast-beating heart.

'Let me get you a drink,' Penny said. 'We're having the Sandfords over as well. You know them, Grady?'

'Yes I do,' he said rather quickly, turning back to the fireplace. 'I have some business connections with Frank Sandford. Is Julia coming with them?'

'She doesn't usually,' Penny replied, returning to Amy's side with two martinis. 'But if she knows that you'll be here this evening then I'm afraid we'll be blighted.'

Amy took her drink with murmured thanks, and surveyed Grady Gilmour over the rim of the glass as she lifted it to her lips. She knew Julia Sandford, and what she knew informed her that this man would be ideal for Julia's particular propensities.

'Well I hope she won't turn up,' Grady said firmly, and for some unaccountable reason Amy's heart beat a trifle faster. 'I met her originally at the Forrest place some months ago, and I had the deuce of a job to keep her off.'

'It's her nature,' Penny said with an impish grin at Amy. 'Come along, do sit down. Amy, how is Jane this evening?'

'I looked in on her as I left the hospital,' Amy replied, moving to a seat and dropping into it. She watched Grady seat himself across the fireplace, lounging back with the easiness he had displayed earlier that afternoon in her office. His eyes were upon her, and Amy was glad that she had taken particular care with her appearance. That was a habit she had lost in the past three years. 'She's making good progress now.'

'I'm the most relieved man in Barnbridge,' Grady said, leaning forward and fixing Amy with a keen stare. 'But I know she's in good hands. I can tell just by looking at you what kind of a person you are, Amy. I couldn't have hoped for a better doctor. I'm changing to your uncle's panel, and I wish you were running his practice with him so I could claim you as the family doctor.'

'You're too kind,' Amy said, her heart lumping heavily in her breast. She tried to catch hold of her rioting emotions, to put them mentally back in their ice boxes, but there was rising excitement inside her, and she felt as if she had just awakened from a Rip Van Winkle sleep. She saw that Penny was watching her closely, and tried to compose her features. Penny knew her well enough to recognise every expression, and she did not want her friend to jump to conclusions. A pulse began to throb in her throat, and she felt heat rise to her cheek. Oh Lord! I'm going to blush! she thought.

The doorbell rang, and Amy was greatly relieved. Penny got to her feet and hurried out of the room, calling over her shoulder:

'I hope Julia is not with them. We want a nice, quiet evening.'

Grady leaned forward, his eyes glinting. There was only a small table lamp alight in one corner of the room. The dancing firelight sent attractive shadows into the corners, and put atmosphere through the room.

'Amy,' he said, 'I want to apologise to you when I get the chance.'

'Why?' She had to force out the word through a suddenly constricted throat.

'I might have hurt your feelings this afternoon,' he replied. 'I asked you if you were married and you said you were not. I'm sorry, but I didn't know about your past. Perhaps I shouldn't have brought it up now. I'm not usually the man to make a mistake. Will you forgive me?'

'There is nothing to forgive, Grady,' she assured him with forced lightness. 'How were you to know?' She had to gulp at the lump which rose in her throat, and her thoughts were thrusting up fragments of crazy impressions. Why should this man affect her in this way? What was there about him that set her pulses leaping and her heart scrambling? She tried to compose herself with thoughts of her dead husband and daughter, but for once there was no heavy pang in the heart, no slashing agony of mind. She breathed with shuddering breath as Penny returned with Frank and Grace Sandford. Was she at last recovering from the awful blow that had smashed her life?

3

Amy drove home later that evening with her head in the clouds. Her impressions of Grady Gilmour were deep set, powerful. She had learned a little about him from the talk of the evening, and found him to be kind hearted, generous and pleasant, not at all like the man she had imagined when Jane Gilmour first came to the hospital. Then she had classed him with all the other business-men who had no time for family life, who lived business twenty-four hours a day. She drove the Mini into the garage and parked it beside her uncle's black Rover. As she went into the house her mind was brimming with new impressions. For three years she had known nothing but the completeness of suffering, and to feel re-awakened like this was like opening the eyes for the first time.

The house was in darkness when she entered, and she made no sound as she went to bed. She was tired, but sleep would not come immediately. Her thoughts were an endless stream, and she relived practically every moment of the evening. But her mind began to close down and finally she drifted into sleep, feeling completely easy for the first time since the tragedy.

The next morning was wet and dismal, but Amy's spirits were high, and she was humming as she went down to breakfast. Aunt Marjorie stared at her in surprise, and Marjorie Davis was not a woman to be easily shaken.

'Amy,' she declared, 'what on earth happened to you? I've never seen you so radiant. Are you feeling well? You're not sickening for anything, are you?'

'I don't think so, Aunt,' Amy replied with a smile. She sighed as she sat down at the table. 'I feel as though a cloud has lifted off my shoulders.'

'That's what an evening out does for you, my dear. You must do it more often. You always did go around quite a bit, and you've been missing that.'

'I've been missing a lot of things, Aunt, but time is still young yet, you know.' She glanced at her watch. 'Time is getting away. Today will be busy. I shall be glad when this evening comes. I never did like ops days.'

'A surgeon's bread and butter!' Marjorie Davis said. 'Now you eat that breakfast I've prepared for you. You're not going off your food, are you?'

'Eating is the last thing I feel like doing,' Amy replied. But she ate a little, and was relieved when she could leave the table and depart for the hospital. She kissed her aunt goodbye and went out to the car. The roads were wet and dangerous, and she drove carefully, arriving in good time. She felt as if she were walking on air as she crossed the park and entered the hospital. There was anticipation inside her, thrilling and bubbling like boiling water. She didn't stop to question this sudden change. She was relieved that the bouts of depression were absent this morning. Despite the rain there appeared to be silver in the heavy clouds.

In her office she checked the morning reports, and was about to start her rounds when the telephone rang. She picked up the receiver, and Grady's voice was in her ear.

'Good morning, Amy,' he said. 'Nice to hear your voice. I hope you won't mind that I called you personally to ask about Jane. But I'm killing two birds with one stone. I know you people are always awfully busy, and I don't want to become a nuisance.'

'You'll never become that,' Amy said swiftly.

'Well that's nice to know.' He laughed, his tones thick and pleasant over the wire.

'If you'll just hang on I'll ring the ward and make an enquiry. I haven't started my round yet.' Amy put down the receiver and used the internal line, calling the children's ward and speaking to Sister Lockwood. She learned that

Jane Gilmour was comfortable, and making progress. She felt relieved as she took up the outside line. 'Hello, Grady, Jane is comfortable. She's making progress, so you can put your mind at rest.'

'Thank you. I shall be in to see her this afternoon. Tell her that, will you, when you see her? I have a business appointment this morning or I'd come over now. Give her my love.'

'Of course.' Amy felt her emotions rippling like water under the caress of a playful breeze. 'You mentioned two birds,' she said. 'I presume that Jane is one and that I'm the other. Is there something else you wanted?'

'Yes, there is.' He paused for a moment, and she could picture his strong face and glinting blue eyes. 'I want the chance to apologise to you for what I said yesterday. That muttered apology last evening isn't the way I usually do things. I'd like to take you out to dinner, and afterwards show you my house. It won't be entirely pleasure, mind you. I want to ask your advice about decorating for Jane's return, and there are some other problems I need to get sorted out. You're the ideal person to help me, if you wouldn't mind.'

'I wouldn't mind in the least,' Amy said, her heart beating heavily. Her throat seemed unaccountably dry, and her fingers were trembling when she lifted a hand to her face.

'You won't be busy this evening? I know a doctor's time is not her own. You seem to be at everyone's beck and call.'

'I shall be free from six onwards, providing there are no unforeseen circumstances.'

'Then may I call for you at seven-thirty?'

'Please do. I shan't keep you waiting.'

She sat down at the desk after he had rung off, and tried to re-collect her wits. Why had she spoken so lightly to him, as if they were friends of long standing? What made her heart act so strangely when she heard his voice or caught a glimpse of him? She was feeling almost lighthearted, and for her that was completely surprising. In the past three years there hadn't been a waking hour that was not crowded with grief.

Amy began her round as if she were walking on air, and she tried to bring her commonsense mind to bear upon her rebelling emotions. But this was a normal reaction. After so long out of the social circle, with nothing but her own morbid thoughts for company, she was a totally friendless creature, lonely and despairing. Only her work had given her comfort, but underneath the grief there had been an aching void that would not be filled by any method of forgetting. The past would not die.

When she came to the children's ward she met Sister Lockwood and, followed by a staff nurse, they went around the patients. Amy had checked several of the young patients before she realized that there were a lot of new soft

toys in the ward. She glanced enquir-
ingly at Sister Lockwood.

'Mr Gilmour sent in a doll for his
daughter, and remembered all the other
patients,' the Sister told her.

'He did?' Amy caught her breath at
mention of his name, and she went
quickly to the next bed, averting her
face from the sharp-eyed Sister. 'He
seems to be a very kind-hearted man,'
she commented.

'Half the nurses in the hospital are
fluttering their eyes at him,' the Sister
said primly, but there was a smile
hovering around her lips. 'He's quite a
handsome man, and as most of the
female staff here are interested in the
daughter, so they're concerned about
the father, but for a different reason.'

Amy suppressed a sigh as she went
on. When she came to Jane Gilmour's
bed she studied the wan face that was
turned up to her. The child's tempera-
ture was down, and Amy was well
pleased. She smiled encouragingly at
the child, but received no response.

'How are you feeling today, Jane?' she asked.

There was no reply, no expression on the youthful face. Amy did not press the child, but as she moved away Sister Lockwood spoke in slow tones.

'She's like that with everyone, Doctor. She won't even speak to her father.'

'I don't think it's anything to worry about,' Amy said. 'She's very ill, and she had quite an ordeal.'

'Do you think her mind could have been affected by her experience?'

Amy surveyed the Sister's concerned features. Then she shook her head.

'We'll watch her closely for signs, of course, but I don't think there will be any mental complications. From what I gather from her father she must have been living under great mental stress for a considerable time, and this escapade of hers was the climax.'

'Anyway, she's making a good recovery from this illness,' Sister Lockwood said. 'I feel so very sorry for the child. All that money in their family and the father can't make the child happy.'

'It's the mother that the child is missing,' Amy said. 'Her father has done everything possible to ensure her happiness, but he can't replace the mother in that child's heart.'

'He could engage someone to take care of her,' Sister Lockwood pursued.

'He's tried that unsuccessfully. So far he's been unable to get the right person.'

Amy was thoughtful as she continued her rounds. She was kept busy through the morning, her mind fully occupied with business, but beneath the routine there was a bubbling sense of anticipation that would not be denied, and at odd moments, when she was relaxing for a time, a picture of Grady Gilmour's face appeared unbidden on the screen of her mind.

During the afternoon she kept expecting to see him appear, for he would come in to visit Jane, but although she remained in her office whenever possible, he did not come, and she was keyed to hear his knock upon the door. Twice during the afternoon there was a heavy knock, that sounded just like his hand, and Amy's heart started fluttering until she knew the identity of the caller. Then, just before it was time to think of calling it a day, the telephone rang. When she answered it Grady spoke into her ear.

'Amy, I'm sorry I couldn't make it to the hospital this afternoon, and I've been trying to find time to ring you to ask you to say a few words to Jane before you leave. She must have been looking for me today. That's business for you. I couldn't even get away to see my sick child. But I've got some very important negotiations going on at this time. Tell her that I love her and I'll see her tomorrow. If there's anything she wants she can tell you and you can let me know this evening. You haven't changed your mind about this evening, have you?'

'Will you be free?' she countered.

'Certainly, and I'd break any business

arrangement just to see you.' There was a lightness in his tones that sent a pang through Amy.

'All right. I was about to leave, but I'll see Jane now and pass on your message.'

'Thanks. See you at seven-thirty.'

The line went dead, and Amy sighed heavily as she replaced the receiver. She wished her heart was not pounding so madly. Even the sound of his voice did things to her. She sat for a moment, deep in thought, and there were pictures of her dead husband and child in her mind. Pain stabbed through her, as sharp as any scalpel, and she breathed deeply, trying to shake off the old familiar nagging of her thoughts. But somehow the degree of agony had lessened. She was surprised by the realization, but it was so. The past was beginning to fade into its proper perspective.

Amy went along to the children's ward with quick steps. She spoke to Sister Lockwood, then entered the ward. Most of the children were quiet now, and she walked softly to Jane Gilmour's bed. The girl was lying with one arm out of the covers, and Amy smiled gently as she replaced it underneath. She stared down into the youthful face, telling herself that in the small heart were pains similar to her own. This child had lost her mother as surely as if she had died. Sympathy spread through Amy. She was old enough to understand what such a loss meant, but a child's mind knew only love and comfort, and there could be no logical reason for a mother's absence to this little one.

She reached out trembling fingers and smoothed back the long fair hair from the feverish forehead. The blue eyes opened and looked up at her, bemused by fever, but showing the emptiness inside, the longing for comfort.

'Mother!' The voice was plaintive, a child's cry from instinct. Amy felt a tugging at her heartstrings. She smiled reassuringly, and caressed the hot forehead.

'Lie quiet, dear,' she soothed. 'You'll soon be feeling better. Would you like a drink?'

There was a slight shake of the head. The wide blue eyes were brimming with tears. Before she could stop the impulse, Amy bent and kissed the flushed cheek.

'I was talking to your daddy a few moments ago,' she said softly. 'He'll be coming to see you tomorrow. Is there anything you would like him to bring?'

'My mother.' The bright eyes were unblinking, and Amy took a long, shuddering breath.

'Perhaps she'll come and see you soon,' she said. 'She doesn't know that you're ill yet, but when she does I'm sure you'll see her.'

'I tried to find her.' The child's voice was weak but harsh. 'But I didn't know where to start looking. Then it got dark and I was afraid.'

'You're quite safe now, Jane. We're

your friends, and we want you to get better quickly. You like the Sister and the nurses, don't you?'

'They're very kind, but I want my mother,' came the heart-rending reply.

'I'll talk to your father tomorrow. You'll look forward to seeing him, won't you?'

'Yes. He's a good father, but Mother didn't love him. She went away. She didn't love me, or she would have taken me with her.'

Two thin arms came out of the blankets and lifted towards Amy, who felt a shuddering of emotion inside her. She smiled tenderly and bent low over the child, putting her gentle hands upon the shaking body. A hot face was pressed against hers, and she felt the wetness of tears on her cheeks. A tiny voice sobbed brokenly. Amy felt tears come into her own eyes. She patted the thin shoulders, soothing the child with words she had not spoken since the death of her own daughter. The thin arms tightened around her neck, reminding her of Susan. There seemed to be a tearing hurt deep inside her, as if cruel fingers were clawing at her heart. She heard the Sister's footsteps coming towards her, and when she looked up her eyes were blurred with tears. She waved urgently, wanting Sister Lockwood to keep away. Crying was the best medicine in the world right now for little Jane Gilmour. She felt relieved when she heard the Sister's footsteps receding, and she soothed the weeping child.

Gradually the sobbing faded, and Amy disengaged herself from the slight arms. The child opened her eyes and stared up at her. Amy patted her shoulder, covering her with the thick blankets.

'There, Jane, you'll feel better in the morning,' she said unsteadily. 'I'll come and see you again. I'm going to see your father this evening. Have you got a message for him? He's very worried about you. He misses your mother too, you know. You're all that he's got left now, and he doesn't want anything bad to happen to you. So you lie here nice and quiet and get well as soon as you can. When you go back home you'll find that everything will be better.'

'I don't like our home,' the girl said. 'It's too big, and I never have anyone to play with.'

'I've spoken to your father about that, and I'm sure he'll make some changes for you, Jane. Shall I tell him that you send your love to him?'

'Yes.' The small head inclined slightly. 'Tell him to come and see me tomorrow.'

Amy settled the child and departed, and Sister Lockwood was waiting for her in the office. Amy took several deep breaths to compose herself. She had been shaken by the child's emotions.

'I'm relieved that she's shown some emotion,' the Sister said. 'That was the best thing that could have happened to her. She's much too small to be bottling up such emotions.'

'Tell the nurses to make as much fuss

of her as they can,' Amy said. 'She's been starved of affection and attention. But I think she's going to be all right when she's recovered from this illness.'

She went wearily back to her office to change, and she found that the display of emotion had drained her of strength. She could feel the child's arms around her neck again, and thought of her own lost daughter. Three years had passed, but the impressions still remained. The pain of it would never go, she knew, and wondered if she had made a mistake in returning to nurse children. Every time she saw a girl of Jane's age she was reminded of Susan, and the grief in her heart had caused wounds which never seemed to heal.

She was in a pensive mood as she drove out of the hospital park, and it still gripped her when she put the car into the garage beside the big house and hurried inside. She knew the purpose of her life had been destroyed, and she had been trying to find another point. She had partly achieved this, but meeting Grady Gilmour had undermined all her built-up defences against grief and loneliness, and now she was restless, disturbed, irritated because she could not pin down the uneasiness. It was as if she was climbing out of a rut, and all the strange new experiences which surrounded her were like impressions gained by a stranger to some place who got the uncanny feeling that she had visited before. It was disconcerting to realize that old, forgotten feelings were returning to the surface of her mind. She had buried them completely, knowing at the time that they could never be resurrected, but Grady Gilmour had proved that miracles still happened, and with a start of awareness she discovered that her uneasiness stemmed from guilt. She had been attracted to Grady Gilmour, and because of her cherished memories of a dead husband she had become guilt-ridden.

The mood seemed to vanish with her acceptance of its cause, and Amy felt almost light-hearted as she went into the kitchen to find her aunt. Wonders never ceased, she thought as she opened the kitchen door. This would be the second night in succession that she had gone out, and it must be a sure sign that her own mind was returning to normal. But her feelings descended sharply when she saw that Tony Walker was in the kitchen with her aunt, and she knew from experience that Tony's presence here so early in the evening presaged an invitation to go out with him. She had always refused, and he knew her reasons, but how would she explain in one breath that she wouldn't go with him but she would be seeing the father of one of her patients?

She was conscious of her changing expression, and was afraid that it showed displeasure. She wouldn't want Tony to think that she was displeased to see him. He had become too great a friend to be offended in any way. But her displeasure was not on account of his presence; rather, it stemmed from the fact that she had to put on an act before him. She disliked concealing her motives, but she could not admit to anyone the way she felt about Grady Gilmour.

4

'Amy,' Tony exclaimed at sight of her, getting to his feet and coming around the table. 'This must be my lucky night. I came on the offchance that you would get home early, and here you are.'

Aunt Marjorie got to her feet and reached for the teapot. Her bright blue eyes were on Amy's face, and the older woman could not fail to notice the changes in Amy's expression and manner. There was animation back in the lovely face after three harrowing years, and Aunt Marjorie did not need to be told that some man had wrought this change, and she also knew the man was not here in the kitchen.

'Tony,' Amy said quickly. 'Before you say any more. Let me say something.' She glanced at her aunt. 'I have to go out tonight.'

'But you were out last night, weren't

you?' Tony blundered, betrayed by his surprise. 'Two nights in a row! This is really something.'

'Last night was a social evening,' Amy said with a faint smile. 'Tonight is something different. It's to do with a patient's welfare.'

'Little Jane Gilmour?' Marjorie Davis enquired.

'Yes. She broke down this evening just before I left. Emotionally, I mean, and it was the best thing that could have happened. I was happy that she chose me to cry on. She's going to be all right now.'

'What's this got to do with her father?' Tony demanded. 'Have you met him yet?'

'I have.' Amy spoke quietly.

'Then there's not much chance for me.' Tony sighed good-naturedly. 'He's something of a ladykiller, Amy, so you'd better watch your step. I don't mean that he chases after the opposite sex, but they seem to go to pieces around him. Julia Sandford is giving him a run for his money at the moment. The poor chap has got his hands full avoiding her. If she gets her hooks into him then he'll be finished. It's all the talk at the club right now. Julia has never concealed her activities around the town, but this time she's pulled out all stops.'

'I don't wish to hear about it, Tony,' Amy said softly.

'Okay. I was just talking. I'll be on my way then.'

'I'm sorry you've had your visit for nothing.' Amy opened the door for him, and he quickly took his leave.

'There's something about you that's different,' Aunt Marjorie said as Amy joined her at the table. 'Is it because of Grady Gilmour?'

'I don't know what you mean, Aunt,' Amy replied severely.

'I know what you have in your heart, dear,' the older woman said compassionately. 'You'll never know the heartache I've had thinking about your plight. But be careful what you do. You might lay yourself open to a lot more trouble.'

'Don't worry about me, Aunt.' Amy spoke lightly, but there was a quiver in her tones. 'It isn't the father who interests me but the child, my patient. She missed her mother so much that she ran away to look for her. I know that kind of feeling. I've been missing my husband and my child for three years. It's something that one cannot explain to a person who has never experienced the same thing. I feel for that child, and she looks so much like Susan.'

'Don't let it become personal, my dear.' There was wisdom in the gently reproving tones. 'You could open up all the old wounds, you know.'

'What makes you think they ever closed?' Amy countered. She smiled as she sipped her tea. 'I need a child to fuss over, to replace this ache I feel in my heart with another child's love. Little Jane Gilmour wants a mother, needs one desperately, and if I can I shall step into the void in her heart.'

'It will be a dangerous thing to do,'

Marjorie Davis said. 'I admire your motives, Amy, but you could do more harm than good.'

'I don't see how.'

'What about your work?'

'It won't suffer. It can't be wrong to want to help a young child recover from a bad emotional upset.'

'No one will ever be able to replace Susan in your heart.'

'I don't have to be told that, Aunt. But it would help me to drive out some of the emptiness. Nothing could make me feel any worse. Just working with children doesn't help. At first I thought it did, but I've realized that the wounds can't be healed. A chance remark, the sight of a child's face, the sound of a girlish voice, all these things can bring it back to the surface. There's no escape, Aunt, and I've learned that. The only thing I can do is try to live with it.'

'I'm sure you're doing that very well,' her aunt said. 'But please be careful, Amy.'

'I've been careful all my life, Aunt.'

Amy smiled wistfully. 'It hasn't done much for me, has it?'

After tea she went to prepare for the evening, and she could not prevent her heart from fluttering when she thought of Grady Gilmour. Did she have a genuine desire to help Jane, or was her emotion aroused by thoughts of the father? She did not know the answer. There was no way of telling.

At seven-thirty she was ready, dressed in a three-quarter lime green coat. She was hatless, her brown hair carefully tended. She waited in her room, not wanting to talk to her aunt, and when she heard the doorbell ring her nerves leaped. She waited for a few moments, then opened her door and went out to the landing to save her aunt from a run up the stairs. Aunt Marjorie paused on the bottom stair, looking up at Amy, a soft light in her blue eyes. She nodded approvingly.

'Mr Gilmour has arrived, dear. I've shown him into the sitting room.'

'Thank you, Aunt.' With her heart

beating faster than ever, Amy descended the stairs.

'Have a nice time, dear. I know you said it was business, but you can enjoy yourself as well, you know.'

'I shall, Aunt, thank you.'

Marjorie Davis went back to the kitchen, her mind filled with hope. Her dearest wish was that Amy would find happiness once again. Amy approached the door of the sitting room with emotion tight in her throat. She threw open the door and stepped across the threshold. Grady Gilmour got up from his seat and came towards her with a smile on his handsome face.

'Hello, Grady,' she greeted. 'You're right on time.'

'The first rule of business,' he replied. 'And you're ready on time. That must be something to write home about. You're very beautiful, Amy. I thought I would have to fight my way through a crowd of admirers, but the house is empty except for your aunt. Don't tell me you're not on the lists of the local men.'

She liked his bluntness, and there was open admiration in his pale eyes. He seemed so tall and broad before her that she felt dwarfed by his size. He took her arm and turned to the door.

'I thought we'd have dinner at 'The Rustic', and afterwards we could go to my place. There's so much I want to talk to you about that I just don't know where to start.'

'You can start by asking me how your daughter is,' she replied.

'Well?' A shadow crossed his face and he seemed to grow tense. 'She's all right, isn't she?'

'She's coming along very nicely.' Amy told him about the incident before she came off duty, and he looked relieved. 'I don't think you'll have any problems when she's on her feet again. I'm going to do all I can to help Jane.' She smiled. 'That doesn't mean that I don't do my best for every patient.'

'You don't have to tell me that,' he said eagerly. 'I've been asking around about you, Amy. I hope you don't mind. I have had nothing but the highest praise come back.'

'I've always done my best,' she admitted.

He closed the sitting room door before she could lead the way out. There was a seriousness in his face that she had not believed he possessed.

'I must touch on the reason I gave for seeing you this evening,' he said without preamble. 'I wonder if I can explain just how I feel over this business with Jane? I've always been up to my neck in work. I thought it was enough for a husband and father to earn enough for his family. I've put a lot of strenuous hours into my business, and somehow the more important things of marriage and home got pushed into the background. I think I can see now why my marriage broke up. But I didn't get the message soon enough. Jane suffered before this all happened. But I've learned my lesson now. Nothing concerning her will be too much trouble. Her slightest wish will be a command to me. I don't give a damn if I spoil her. It's been a shock to me, looking up from business and taking a good squint at life around me. My daughter was a poor little rich girl! I only hope that I'm not too late to repair the damage. I've already made a start to put matters right. I'm taking more time off work. I'll see more of Jane when she gets out of hospital. She's going to lead a more normal life, and I don't care what it costs me. But I'm getting away from the point. How can I tell you what I feel for you? This upset that shocked me back to my senses is as nothing compared with what you must have suffered. You lost your whole family in that tragedy. I wish I had known about it before I opened my big mouth.'

'But you didn't say anything to be sorry for,' Amy said helplessly, almost overwhelmed by his fervour. 'It's life, you know. I'm not shrugging off all the agony with a casual statement, but that's a fact. These things come along and we have to face up to them.'

'I thought I was in the centre of a tragedy when my wife walked out on me,' he countered. 'But I still had Jane, and I was too much of a fool to see that. I think that in my mind I even began to blame her for what happened. She tied Marion to the house. But it wasn't her fault. It was mine, and her mother's selfishness.'

'It's not too late to put matters right in your life,' Amy said. 'That's a blessing.'

'That's why I can feel the tragedy that hit you,' he replied. 'But sympathy is no use. Words can't help, can they? One has to live with it until it becomes habit and loses its sharpness.'

'You sound as if you know something about it,' Amy remarked.

'Not to the extent you suffered, Amy,' he replied grimly. 'Come along, let's be going. I'm getting much too fervent about this. My emotions are undergoing something of a change. I became really hard after Marion left me, but this business with Jane has altered me a lot.'

They left the house, and Grady's big Bentley stood at the kerb. He opened the door for her, helped her into the seat, and closed the door with a bang. She watched his big figure as he walked around the car. He was a man sure of himself, and with his business record she didn't wonder that he oozed self-confidence. He drove fast, negotiating the traffic with the skill of a man accustomed to using his judgement in all matters. Amy settled back in the seat, content to watch him. His profile was handsome, and she liked the line of his jaw, the straight angle of his nose. His nostrils were flared a little, showing something of the fighter that he was. She put his age at about thirty-five. There was a streak or two of grey at his temples, but in the main there was something boyish about his fair hair, which he kept cut short.

'The Rustic' was the biggest hotel in Barnbridge, standing opposite the railway station. It was a substantial building, showing the craftsmanship of a bygone age. The exterior was of dark stone, typically Victorian, but Amy knew the interior had been recently renovated, and at great cost. There were five storeys to the building, and in the summer the roof garden was an ideal spot for sunbathing and cool drinks.

Grady parked the car behind the hotel, and he took Amy's arm possessively as they walked around to the front entrance.

'I haven't been in here since the modernisation,' she said, greatly conscious of his nearness. He had a powerful magnetism about him, and she could feel it tugging at her awareness. There were tiny prickles of ice jagging along her spine as they walked through the ornate doorway and crossed a wide expanse of dark red carpet. He kept the fingers of his right hand gripped tightly around her elbow. Amy tried not to remember the fact that the last time she had been in here her husband had been with her. She could remember that night clearly.

Memory was such a curse when there were tragic incidents in the past.

'I come here often,' he remarked. 'Entertaining business associates is a great part of business today. Times have changed a lot in the last fifty years.'

A waiter appeared and escorted them to a table set in an alcove by a window. Soft lights were dispelling the shadows, and Amy was struck by the smooth atmosphere encouraged by the decor. But she thought she liked it better as it used to be, and knew that she was a sentimental, unrealistic romantic.

'You're looking happy this evening,' Grady remarked gently. 'I expect I'm right when I assume that you don't go out much, eh?'

'Perfectly right,' she replied. Her eyes were glowing, her voice unsteady, and there was no reason to hide her delight. 'But three years are little enough time in which to mourn the loss of a family.' She felt a twinge of grief, but forced it away. Nothing must spoil the pleasure of this evening. She wanted a perfect memory to retain, something with which to fight back against the black thoughts that often invaded her mind. She had no happy memories now, no ammunition to use in her ceaseless fight against grief. But she was making headway, however imperceptible. The fact that she was here with a man proved it.

The meal was splendid, and with her heightened emotions, she had never enjoyed food more. A light wine put colour into her cheeks and twin spots of light into her dark eyes. A waiter brought coffee. Amy was transported by the experience. Now she could realize just how narrow her world had become, and what she had thought stimulating and worthwhile before this evening seemed unbearable, intolerable compared with this incident. Her escort was a man of impeccable taste and good manners, but it was just an incident to him, she thought. An ordinary evening out with the woman who was taking care of his child.

But he didn't act as if it were so. He smiled and listened to her chatter. He was the perfect companion, guiding their conversation along general lines, telling her what she wanted to hear, maintaining a comfortable atmosphere, and Amy felt a pang of regret when he finally called for the bill, settled it, and then helped her out of her chair.

They left the hotel and went around to the car park. There was a chill breeze, and Amy shivered as she waited for him to unlock the car. Clouds were scurrying through the night sky, obscuring the stars, adding to the darkness, and she thought her life was symbolised by the bright, warm atmosphere inside the hotel and this darkness, cold and dreary, outside. She was always on the outside now, able to see the joy and happiness of others but unable to participate. She was one of the world's spectators, shut out, exiled by the tragedy that had overtaken her family.

She climbed into the car and sat still and cold, frozen by her memories. Why did they have to surge up in her mind and spoil her only pleasure? The emptiness and desolation seemed unbearable, and she sighed heavily. Grady glanced at her, guessing at the nature of her thoughts, but he spoke lightly, hoping to guide her back to the lights of pleasure.

'I think you've enjoyed yourself this evening,' he said. 'You should get out more, Amy. Life is too short to be spent shut away from anything. Experiences such as yours have to be fought all the way, don't they? I think you've made good progress against your particular ogres.'

'Yes. It's been a struggle.' Amy smiled to herself. 'I have had a wonderful evening. Thank you very much for taking pity on me.'

'It was nothing of the sort,' he retorted quickly. 'I was selfish in my motives, don't you worry. I'm a hard-headed businessman, and my kind never do a thing for nothing. I want your experience and skill for my daughter. I've taken you out to dinner, made you briefly happy, and now I want to be repaid.'

He spoke lightly, and she glanced at his dark profile. He was driving steadily, and she recognised the route. They were going to the better part of town, where the richer folk lived on and around Pent's Hill.

'I'm ready to help you any way I can,' she replied. 'But I don't think you'll have any problems with Jane when she comes home. Just see to it that she doesn't get lonely again. It's all right to hire the best in nurses and governesses, but a child can so easily get lonely.'

'Like an adult,' he retorted softly. 'Loneliness is one of the curses of society. Everyone is too busy making a life for himself and his family that he hasn't time to look out for others. There are exceptions, of course, such as you.' He glanced at her, his face sombre in the reflected glare from the headlights. 'It usually takes some tragedy to make a person think deeply about life and its meaning.' He fell silent, as if aware that he was talking in a dangerous direction.

Amy thought about Jane Gilmour, and could still feel the child's arms around her neck. She smiled tenderly. Now she could not remember what her own child's arms had been like. It was a tragedy in itself that time should wipe away some of the memories. The sharpness of her pain was almost gone. Time blunted everything with its inexorable passing, and that was something for which to be thankful.

Grady turned the big car into a wide driveway, and gravel grated under the spinning wheels. Tall trees lined the drive, interlocking their stark branches overhead. The house was in darkness, a huge black mass in the shadows, but as the car halted in front of the steps leading to the massive door, a lamp came on over the doorway, throwing pale yellow light upon the steps.

'The house looked deserted, didn't it?' Grady demanded as he opened the car door for her. 'I never like to see it in the darkness. It always reminds me of a dead house. I like plenty of light.'

The door was opened as they ascended the four wide steps, and an oldish woman peered out at them.

'Edith, this is Doctor Merrill. She's taking care of Jane at the hospital.'

'How is Jane?' the housekeeper asked as she took Amy's coat.

'She's much better now,' Amy replied. 'In a week she'll be greatly recovered.'

'Doctor Merrill is going to advise me on the way a young girl should be brought up,' Grady said. 'Is the fire alight in the library, Edith?'

'Yes. Is there anything you want?'

'No thanks. I'll ring if there should be something.' Grady took Amy's arm, and she experienced that shuddering sensation as he led her along the long, wide hall. 'I'm not going to show you around the house tonight,' he remarked. 'It's too cold in some of these rooms, and the daylight is needed to do justice to the place. When you get some time off you must come up and have a look around.'

'I should love to,' Amy replied.

Grady opened a door and switched

on a light. He ushered her into a library which was tastefully furnished. There was comfort here, she saw, and sight of the big fire burning in the huge grate reminded her that she was feeling cold. They walked to the fireplace, and Amy glanced at the shelves of books.

'Do you read much?' she demanded.

'Not now,' he told her, moving to a cabinet and lifting the lid. 'Would you like a drink? I used to read quite a lot when I was younger, but business is a jealous god.' He poured drinks as he spoke, then came across to stand beside Amy, handing her a glass filled with amber liquid. 'I suppose your work keeps you pretty busy. You're like me, you don't have set times.'

'I'm thankful for the work,' she told him. 'It helps to keep the thoughts at bay.'

They were silent for a moment, and Amy raised her glass to her lips, study-ing him over the rim. Her dark eyes were keen and probing. He was a hand-some man, and from their conversation of the evening she knew he had problems on his mind. His daughter occupied him most at the moment, because he had been badly shocked by her behaviour. But Amy didn't think he would push her into the background again. He had come to realize that she was a person, someone who depended upon him for her life itself. She was not just a responsibility but someone who needed love and protection, and she could tell by his manner that Jane Gilmour's troubles were over. She would find an affectionate parent when she returned home.

'Do you think I should send Jane away to a boarding school?' Grady asked suddenly, and his blue eyes were filled with question as he studied Amy. 'She would be mixing with children, and I think that's what she needs.'

'I don't think so.' Amy was doubtful. 'What she needs right now is someone she really knows. If she went away to school she would be among strangers. I wouldn't advise it so soon, anyway. Give her a chance to settle back here.

Let her know that you love her. That will give her confidence.'

'I'll do all of that,' he said firmly. 'Poor little girl. Can you imagine what her life has been like, living in this great temple of a house with no one but the servants to take care of her? She rarely saw me, and then only briefly. I'm not surprised by what's happened, in retrospect, but I have been a blind fool not to have seen it coming.'

'So long as it isn't repeated,' Amy said softly. 'I've taken a liking to Jane, Grady. She reminds me a lot of my own dead child. I should like to do what I can for her when she is better.'

'Of course,' he said eagerly. 'That's what I was trying to lead up to. I know you're admirably suited to handling children. I sensed it the moment I set eyes on you at the hospital. You're missing a child's love and Jane is missing a mother. It's obvious that you both can help each other. Am I presuming too much, Amy?'

'No,' she replied. 'I think it will work

all right. If Jane does take to me then I'll cultivate her friendship. She needs a lot of help, and if I can get her on my side before we start then it will be a great advantage.'

The telephone rang before he could reply, and Grady pulled a face as he strode across the room. Amy watched him as he picked up the receiver. He was so confident and sure in his manner. She turned to the fire, staring into the leaping flames while he took his call, but she could not help overhearing what he said.

'Hello,' he said into the mouthpiece. 'This is Grady Gilmour. Yes. That's right, I have been out all evening and I'm back early. No, you can't come over and see me. I have a friend here. I told you earlier that I couldn't see you. Goodbye.'

He hung up, and Amy turned from the fire as he returned to her side. He had spoken gently on the phone, but there was a hard expression on his face as he glanced at her.

'That was Julia Sandford,' he said. 'She's becoming a nuisance, chasing after me. How does one put off a girl without offending her father?' He shook his head. A sigh gusted from him. 'What one has to do in the name of business,' he muttered. 'When I had Marion she kept all other females off my neck. I shan't go looking for another wife, though, just to save myself that kind of trouble. I might jump out of the frying pan into the fire.'

His gaze lifted to hold Amy's eyes, and she smiled consolingly.

'I'd better take you home,' he said. 'It's getting late. At least I know where I am with you, Amy. You've got the makings of a good friend. I hope you and Jane will get along all right together. But time will tell.'

Amy agreed, but she didn't care for the label he had attached to her. She felt more than friendship in her heart for this man, although she tried to quell it. Complication was the last thing they needed.

She was silent and thoughtful on the drive home, and he did not interrupt her. When he brought the big car to a halt at the kerb in front of the house she felt reluctance seep into her, but she turned to him with a smile.

'Thank you for a wonderful evening,' she said. 'It's been quite an experience.'

'I have a lot to thank you for,' he responded. 'But if it meant so much to you then I shall be pleased to see you again. Would that fit in well with your duties?'

'Yes, so long as you let me know in advance.'

He took her hand, holding it tightly for a moment. He stared into her face, searching for something that did not show in her expression.

'Amy, you've restored some of my faith in the female of the species,' he told her. 'I'll see you at the hospital tomorrow when I come to see Jane. Give her my love in the morning, will you?'

'Of course. She's a special patient.'

She watched him get out of the car and walk around to open the door for her, and he accompanied her to the door of the house. He was holding her elbow again, and Amy could feel spasms of emotion jerking through her breast.

'Goodnight,' he said huskily. 'Thanks for your company.'

Amy opened the door and stepped across the threshold. When she turned to look at him he was departing, and she smiled as he turned to wave. Then he was gone, the big car purring away into the night. She closed the door with a sigh, and some of the old black thoughts came seeping back into her mind. She felt something like Cinderella returning to the kitchen, and the magic of the evening frittered away before the onset of the old routine of her mental pattern. But there was a tiny spark in her soul that did not die. She cherished it, tried to nourish it with her thoughts, and when she went to bed she felt easier than she had done for many months . . .

5

The next few days passed quickly, her routine at the hospital merely a necessary interlude in her suddenly valuable time. Amy began to find that her spirits were riding high, like a kite on a windy day. She spent more time than she should have done with Jane Gilmour, and each passing day saw a greater change in the child's condition. After the first few days Jane began to recover from her shyness, and by the end of the week the child was always impatiently waiting to set eyes on Amy. The change in the girl's manner was so marked that Sister Lockwood remarked upon it.

'You've got just the right touch with that child, Doctor Merrill. You've brought her out of herself. I thought we were in for some trouble when I first saw her, but she's acting almost normally now.'

'She's got some scars on her soul and

some shadows in her eyes,' Amy replied, 'but I think the worst of it is over. I think we'll be able to discharge her some time next week.'

Grady Gilmour came into the hospital to see his daughter, and never missed calling at Amy's office. As she got to know him better, Amy realized that she was falling in love with him. His manner towards her was always courteous and friendly, but there seemed to be a barrier between them, something intangible, powerful enough to hold him at a respectful distance. Amy didn't notice it at first, but it gradually made its presence felt. He didn't ask her out during that second week, but she knew he was extremely busy. Some new deals that he had mentioned were nearing completion, and even when he was with her in the office his mind seemed busy on something else.

He was more than pleased with his daughter's progress, and Amy was relieved that no apparent complications were arising. He was so happy now, with his newfound responsibility, and Amy thought that Jane would benefit greatly from her father's fresh awareness.

On the following Friday afternoon Grady came to the office, and when Amy opened the door to him he grinned, stifling a sigh.

'I haven't had much time to see anything of you, have I?' he demanded, sitting down in the seat beside the desk. 'It's the same kind of thing that alienated my ties with Marion, and Jane. But thank God I've managed to get back on the old footing with Jane. She's coming along nicely, and she's full of talk about you. I'm glad about that, Amy. When can she come home?'

'Next week, about Wednesday, I think,' Amy said. 'The change in her manner is remarkable. I'm just hoping now that going back to that big house of yours won't throw her into that former despair.'

'I'm worried about that,' he confessed. 'Have you got any thoughts on the subject? Is there anything I can do to prevent a recurrence?'

'I'll talk to her over the next few days,' Amy said. 'She's beginning to tell me everything. I've gained her confidence, and that was the most important thing.'

'I've had to promise her that you'll come and spend a few days with us,' he said. 'Is that an impossibility, Amy?'

'I don't know.' She looked at him, their gazes holding. Amy felt her heart start pounding.

'It would be for the good of the patient,' he pushed. 'I think you should seriously consider it. Jane is such a sensitive girl, and you've captured her attention. That's what you wanted in the first place, you said. So what happens now?'

'I've got some holidays due,' Amy said slowly. 'I suppose I could take them and spend them with Jane.'

'Have you not made any other arrangements?' he demanded.

'I never make arrangements now,' she replied with a smile.

He studied her face, nodding his

head slowly. When she said no more he got to his feet.

'I've got some more business to attend to,' he said, sighing. 'When am I going to take you out again, Amy? I enjoyed our first evening.'

'Whenever you wish,' she replied.

'Good. What about tomorrow evening. Same time?'

'I shall look forward to it,' Amy told him.

After he had gone she tried to analyse her feelings, but she could not find the thoughts that would lay bare the vibrant emotions at work inside her. She was restless, too, and left the office to visit Jane Gilmour.

The child was happy, with clear blue eyes that had lost the shadows of the illness and her suffering. She smiled at Amy, who sat down on the foot of the bed.

'Well, Jane, how are you feeling now?'

'I'm much better thank you. My father came to see me this afternoon. He brought me this.' She lifted a small musical box from under the covers, and when she lifted the lid Amy heard a Viennese waltz being played.

'Why, that's beautiful!' she declared. 'You are a lucky girl to have a father who brings such lovely gifts. Are you looking forward to going home?'

'Do I have to go yet?' A shadow crossed the child's face.

'Not for another week, but you're getting much better, and we shall need this bed for another child who is ill.'

'I shall miss you, Doctor Amy.'

The words stabbed straight through Amy's heart. She smiled and reached out a friendly hand and patted the child's shoulder.

'No you won't, because I've been talking to your father, and he's asked me to come and spend a few days with you.'

'Has he really?' The light that shone from the girl's eyes was a pleasure to see, and again Amy was reminded of her own daughter.

'Yes, so you hurry up and get really

well and go home, then I'll come and stay with you.'

'But it will only be for a few days, then I shall be on my own again,' Jane said.

'We'll have to think of something for you,' Amy told her. 'You'll be going to school after a week or two convalescent.'

'I don't go to school. I have a governess.'

'So you've never mixed with other children!' Amy shook her head. No wonder this child had broken down! She had been completely isolated. 'Well, we'll see what can be done.'

'I asked father about my mother, and he told me she wouldn't be coming. I don't really want her because she didn't want me.'

'But you ran away to find her,' Amy said. 'You wanted her then.'

'I wanted someone, and she was the only one I could think of.'

'Well you won't be lonely again,' Amy promised her. 'I'll come and see you sometimes. I once had a little girl like you, and I miss her in the way that you miss your mother. So you see, we can help each other.'

'Father told me about your little girl. I am sorry for you. I like you, Doctor Amy.'

'And I like you, Jane. Now you lie nice and quiet. Your tea will be here soon. I have some more work to do, but I'll come and see you again before I go off duty.'

'Don't forget,' Jane Gilmour called after her, and Amy turned, smiled and waved.

Amy was beginning to realize that her mind had changed imperceptibly in the past few days. Since the tragedy she had been introverted with grief, but the coming of Jane and Grady Gilmour into her life had made the necessary difference to start her thinking above her present narrow horizons. She was getting back to normal after a vacuum of three years. The unreality of grief was fading. In Jane Gilmour she had found a new interest, which was exactly what her mind needed. They could help each other, she thought, nodding to herself. A child who had lost her mother needed love and companionship, and a mother who had lost her daughter wanted another daughter upon which to lavish the frustrated love and affection inside her.

She went back to see the child as she went off duty, and her heart was warmed by the eagerness showing in Jane Gilmour's face as the child greeted her. Some kind of natural magic had been at work on the both of them, Amy thought. The child was replacing the lost mother with another figure, and it was a sign to Amy that the danger for Jane was over. She stayed quite some time with the child, and then reluctantly took her leave, promising to see the girl next morning. Heaven seemed to open for her when Jane lifted up both arms, and Amy bent over the small figure, feeling the thin arms entwining around her neck as if they would never let go.

As she drove home later she tried to

analyse her thoughts. She was worrying subconsciously about the girl's discharge from hospital. Returning to the surroundings where her troubles had originated might have an adverse effect upon Jane Gilmour that would not show until damage had been done. But there seemed to be no other alternative. The return home might be eased slightly if Amy took a hand. She had some days due to her, and by accompanying Jane to that big house on Pent's Hill trouble might be averted. The thought of spending some time under Grady Gilmour's roof appealed to her, but it was not for that reason she decided to go through with it.

Aunt Marjorie was waiting for her when she got in. Grady Gilmour had telephoned to say that he had to go to London for a few days. Amy thought about their date for the next evening, and smiled wryly. But she was concerned over Jane, and knew that her own feelings would have to wait. She ate her tea almost mechanically, her mind on other things. Her aunt hovered around in the background, and Amy suddenly became aware of the older woman's tension. She looked up, her keen brown eyes taking in the worry on Aunt Marjorie's face.

'Aunt, there's something the matter,' she said quickly.

'There is?' A shadow crossed the woman's face. 'Then tell me about it, dear.'

'Not from my point of view, but from yours. I can see it in your face. What's on your mind?'

'It's nothing but concern for you, Amy.' Aunt Marjorie came to the table and sat down. Amy poured two fresh cups of tea. For a moment there was silence. Then the older woman nodded. 'I've seen a change in you this past week, Amy. It's what I've been waiting for. You're finally recovering from the tragedy. But you must be careful how you act until you become accustomed to the change. You're like a child now, a young girl emerging from childhood, with everything new and strange and all the emotions yet to be experienced. I hope you won't get hurt. I know where your feelings are lying right now.'

'What are you trying to say, Aunt? There's no need to beat around the bush with me, is there?'

'I'm not beating around the bush. I'm just finding it difficult to put what's in my mind into the right words. You're becoming interested in Grady Gilmour. Perhaps it is the child in hospital that's attracted you. But you can get hurt, and badly. In your present state of mind a setback could do permanent harm to your emotions. You're still a young woman, Amy, and I beg you to be careful.'

'Aunt, most of your fears are groundless. There is something in what you say, I admit, but I can't get hurt. Anyway, Grady Gilmour is a gentleman. But it is little Jane that I'm worried about. She'll be discharged soon, and she'll be going back to the environment that started all her troubles. I am in a bit of a quandary, Aunt. I've half promised to take a few days' holiday when she goes home, and to spend them with her.'

'You need something to fill that emptiness in your heart,' Aunt Marjorie said slowly, 'but you must think of the child, Amy. If you take her mother's place in her heart you'll have to remain there until she's old enough to stand on her own emotions. You know that, don't you?'

'I know it, Aunt, and that's what is worrying me. I shouldn't want the child to get hurt. She's only seven, and she's going to need a woman to lean on for a good many years. I could so easily be that woman, and I need someone like her to help me over the next few difficult years. Do you think I shall be doing the right thing by trying to step into her mother's shoes?'

'It depends how far you intend going.'

'You mean with Grady Gilmour, don't you?'

'Yes. He's not an old man, is he? Supposing he decides to remarry? What happens then? His next wife might not like the idea of a female in the background, playing mother to her stepdaughter.'

'I see.' Amy sighed deeply. 'I never thought about that side of it.' She shook her head. She was in love with Grady, and she could not see him remarrying. From the way he spoke at times she thought he might remain single for the rest of his life.

'You know what it would do to the child if you filled her heart for a short time, then had to leave her,' Aunt Marjorie said.

'Yes. It would break her completely. She's a highly sensitive child.'

'It isn't so easy to help people in this world, is it?' There was wisdom in the older woman's voice. 'Amy, I want to see you happy. I want you to do the right thing, but don't ask me what that right thing is. Something always seems to go wrong when mere humans try to play God. That's what you're about to do, and all I ask is that you think long and carefully about it before you take the step. There'll be no turning back for you once you accept the responsibility of filling that child's life.'

'I know.' Amy spoke softly. 'But I need her as much as she needs me.'

'And the father? Where does he enter into your calculations?'

'Grady?' Amy smiled. 'I'm in love with him, Aunt. I have a feeling that he might be attracted to me, but all that is in the future. Life is a gamble, just the plain living of it, and we have to take everything on trust from the cot to the grave.'

'I hope it will work out for you, dear.' Aunt Marjorie reached across the table and took Amy's hand. 'You deserve happiness, and I've prayed these past few years, I can tell you. But take some advice from an old woman who's seen too much trouble in her time. If you make a mistake it won't be just yourself who will get hurt.'

The doorbell rang, and Amy got quickly to her feet. She held Aunt

Marjorie's gaze as she went around the table, and there was tacit understanding between them. Amy went to answer the door, and found Tony Walker on the step.

'Hello, Amy,' he said. 'Are you busy this evening?'

'No. Come in, Tony.'

He stepped across the threshold, tall and handsome, and Amy found herself comparing him with Grady. Her heart seemed to ache when she thought of Grady. Tony's blue eyes regarded her intently.

'I'm all dressed up and nowhere to go,' he said. 'Can I entice you out for the evening?' He smiled. 'I know you've started out of your shell, so don't give me the old excuses anymore.'

She smiled. 'I don't feel much like going out,' she replied, 'but if you insist then I'll go with you.'

'Whatever's happening?' he demanded jocularly. 'The age of miracles is past, and yet you're waving the wand over me.'

'Do you want to go out?' she asked.

'Would you rather sit in and play chess?' he countered. 'You're not that old, Amy.'

'Age doesn't enter into it,' she replied, and his face was instantly serious.

'I know, and that's the hell of it. You've got yourself hooked with Grady Gilmour, haven't you?'

'I think so.'

'Then I shouldn't be here asking you out.' He smiled, but there was no mirth in him. 'We're handling all Gilmour's business, and I shouldn't want to do anything to affect that. He could be nasty if he found out that I was seeing you behind his back.'

'Tony, you're being absurd, and you know it,' Amy told him severely.

'Am I?' He nodded. 'All's fair in love or war, Amy. So what are you going to do this evening? Won't you take pity on someone who is becoming a stranger to you?'

'That's not true, Tony. You don't

think like that, do you?'

'That's precisely how my brain is working at the moment.' He smiled to belie his words, but there was an intentness in his eyes that told Amy he was not merely joking. Her heart seemed to miss a beat as she studied his face, and she knew she did not want to hurt him. He had been a good friend during the dark months that stretched behind her.

'If you'll give me fifteen minutes,' she said. 'But I'd like to know where you intend taking me.'

'There's a small party at Jack Foster's place. You know Jack. He's a chartered accountant. We're quite friendly, and he asked me to drop by. Jack is rapidly becoming the centre man of the new social set that's springing up in Barnbridge.'

'I wouldn't know anything about that,' Amy retorted. 'I've been out of touch for years, and I don't particularly feel inclined to go back to that round of living.'

'Amy, you're turning positively antisocial,' he said with a grin. 'But if you don't want to go to Jack's then I suggest we take a drive and stop at some little pub for a drink and a chat.'

'What do we have to talk about?' There was a smile on Amy's lips as she watched his face for expression.

'All right. So we'll sit here at home and talk, and drink your uncle's sherry.' He laughed good-naturedly. 'You really are the limit, Amy.'

She was serious for a moment, pausing in her turn to the kitchen. Her brown eyes were glinting as she regarded him, and she saw the query that filled his intent expression.

'Tony, why don't you find yourself a nice girl and get married and settle down?' she demanded.

'I don't think you have any right to ask me that question,' he countered, and his lips tightened as he kept his eyes upon her face. 'Anyway, are you trying to tell me that you are not a nice girl? You're the only one I'm keeping company with.'

'That's a quaint phrase,' she retorted.

'I expect it came out of one of your law books.'

'Something like that. Now go and change while you're still in the mood to go out. I'll talk to your aunt while I'm waiting for you. Is she in the kitchen?'

'Yes. Help yourself. I shan't be long.'

Amy went up to her room and began to change. She didn't feel much like going out. She would have to be up early in the morning to get to the hospital, and she thought about Jane Gilmour as she prepared for the evening. Poor little girl! Something had to be done for her. It wasn't just for the child's sake, though, and she knew it. There was something inside her crying out for succour, and only the love and dependence of a child could satiate the emotion. Her own dead child had left a great gap. Grady came into it as well, and she knew it, although she tried to keep the thought from growing into a recognisable state of mind. If she admitted it definitely to herself she would have no rest, no peace of mind until matters came to a conclusion, and there was no way of knowing what that end would be. She could not force the issue, and she was putting her future happiness and peace of mind in the balance by taking the chance that everything would work out all right.

But life was a gamble, as she had remarked to Aunt Marjorie, and she had to take the chance. Someone needed her help, and it was only natural that she hoped to get something out of the ultimate situation. Whether it would turn out to her satisfaction was a matter totally out of her hands, but if trying was needed to make it come right then she had nothing to worry about. She would do the trying, and then some . . .

6

Tony was exuberant as he drove her through the town. They had not been out together for quite some time, and he knew that he had been losing the fight to gain her love. Since Grady Gilmour appeared on the scene the signs had been very plain. But Tony was not fool enough to imagine that Amy's presence with him now was a sign in his favour. He knew she was recovering from the tragedy of three years before, and she still had a long way to go before she was completely recovered. He was in love with her, and felt that she had some feeling for him. He knew he would have to wait some time before she would be ready for a serious proposal, and sensed that if he mistimed his approach he would be turned down out of hand.

Amy sat silent at his side as he sent

the car towards the outskirts. She was thinking of Grady Gilmour. She had been looking forward to an evening out with him, but his business in London came first, and there would be plenty of time to see him when she went to the house on Pent's Hill with Jane. She thought of the child, now asleep in her hospital bed, and emotion filtered through her. There was so much she wanted to do for the girl, but she was afraid that her thoughts of Grady would influence her actions, and she didn't want Jane to suffer. If she was afraid that Grady might fall in love again and marry then her attitude to the girl would be coloured by that fear. She would be chary of starting an association with Jane because a parting later would only reproduce the girl's present suffering, only in a greater degree.

'Penny for them,' Tony said at length.

'They're not worth anything,' she replied, stirring herself. 'Where are we?'

'About six miles out of town, and going north. This is a fine chance for me to talk seriously to you, Amy. I've been wanting to for quite some time, but I can't judge the right moment. I think you're more amenable to conversation now than you have ever been during our friendship.'

'Thank you.' She glanced at him, seeing his taut expression, and wondered if he planned to propose to her. She couldn't face that this evening. 'What do you call serious conversation?'

'I should like to know what your future plans are.'

'How they might affect you?'

'Something like that. Grady Gilmour has become important to you, hasn't he?'

'His daughter has,' she countered, and said no more. A silence developed, and Tony didn't know what to say to break it. He suppressed a sigh, realizing that she was going to be difficult, and he decided that it wasn't the right moment to talk of what lay in his heart.

'Would you like a drink?' he asked at last.

'Yes please. There's a little pub about two miles along here.'

'Yes, the 'Dog and Duck',' he supplied. 'When was the last time you were here?'

'Before the flood,' she told him, smiling thinly. 'It's too far back to remember. What's on your mind, Tony? I'll rather know now than suffer your tension.'

'Does it show as much as that?' he demanded. He took a deep breath. 'But it doesn't matter. Now isn't the time to broach it anyway.'

He drove on at greater speed, sensing that he had reached a critical moment and wanting it to pass without too much damage to his plans. They saw the lights of the pub ahead, and he drove into the car park. There were almost a score of cars there, and he remembered with a curse that this place had become popular with a lot of his friends. They often motored out during the evening for a drink and a game of darts. He didn't want to walk in on them tonight; least of all tonight. As Amy opened her door to get out he touched her elbow.

'Let's go somewhere else,' he pleaded. 'This place looks as if it might be crowded.'

'You want to go somewhere quiet, so you can talk seriously?' Amy shook her head. 'No, Tony, don't do it. I should hate to spoil a good friendship by throwing cold water on your plans. We could never be the same old friends if you proposed to me and I turned you down.'

'I can wait,' he said hopefully. 'Okay, so we'll go in here. It'll be noisy, boisterous, but if you don't mind then we'll have a good evening's entertainment.'

Amy nodded and opened the door, slipping out into the darkness. A cold breeze tugged at her hair, and she hurried around the car, reaching Tony's side as he locked his door. He took her arm and almost ran her towards the squat building. She was aware that his touch failed to awaken her as Grady's had done. She was breathing hard as they entered the little pub, and Tony ushered her into the lounge. They paused on the threshold, and Tony saw several of his personal friends among the two dozen people present. There was a good deal of chatter going on, and several voices greeted them. Amy looked around almost nostalgically. It had been a long time since she had been here. It had been in another lifetime, she thought, and felt a dark pang of emotion stab through her breast. She took a deep breath and smiled as she recognised some of the faces. Tony took her across to an empty table and she sat down. He went across to the bar to order their drinks, and she sat looking at faces and listening to the many conversations.

This place hadn't altered at all, she thought. It was only people who changed, or the situations one encountered. She was here with Tony, and the last time she had entered the place her husband had been with her. That was the only difference. She was still the same, except inside, and her husband was dead, but the same man was behind the bar, and some of the same faces were here. It was as if they had never been away, as if they had waited here for her return.

When Tony returned to the table several of his friends came across for a chat, and Amy found herself drifting into the old, almost forgotten channels. A native of Barnbridge, she knew almost everyone by sight, and they knew her. They also knew about her personal tragedy, and they were pleased to see her out and about again after so long in the limbo of bereavement.

After several drinks she felt easier, and was smiling and responding to Tony's cheerful manner. As the evening drew on even more patrons arrived, and the lounge became very crowded. Amy was beginning to look at the clock on the wall, and Tony was trying not to read significance into her actions, but he could tell by her expression that it was time to go, and he wanted this evening to go on forever. He was about to suggest that they started home when Amy glanced towards the door as it was opened. He followed her gaze, and his lips pulled taut when he saw Grady Gilmour and Julia Sandford standing on the threshold.

A quick glance at Amy's face showed him the exact state of her mind, and he felt a twinge of pity for her, but at the same time his hopes soared. He knew she was halfway to being in love with Gilmour, and he knew that Julia Sandford was chasing him for all her worth. He could suddenly see a neat ending to a situation which was beginning to baffle him. If Julia managed to get her claws into Gilmour then it was feasible that Amy would turn for solace to the man nearest her. He was that man, and he didn't care how it came about, so long as he and Amy came together.

'I thought Gilmour was going to London.' He leaned across the table to speak to her.

Amy nodded, her eyes intent upon

128

the two in the doorway. Grady was looking around, and when their eyes met Amy saw the surprise that came to his handsome face. He spoke to Julia Sandford, who glanced in their direction, and the next moment Grady was leading the girl across to their table. Amy saw that most of the other tables were fully occupied, and she breathed deeply as Tony got to his feet.

'Hello, Gilmour, Julia,' Tony greeted. 'You can have our table. We were just leaving.'

'Stay and have a drink with us,' Grady said, his eyes on Amy. 'I'm surprised to see you here. What will you have?' He glanced at her glass, smiled, and started for the bar. 'I'll make it the same again,' he called over his shoulder.

Julia glanced at Tony, who pulled out a chair for her, and as she sat down the girl let her brown eyes study Amy's face.

'I must say you're a stranger around town,' she said. 'Where have you been hiding yourself?'

129

'Some people do work, Julia,' Tony said quickly. 'You know that Amy is a doctor at the hospital, and she leads a more hectic life than you.'

'I doubt that,' the girl replied coolly. 'You've got Grady's daughter in your care, haven't you?' She didn't wait for an answer. 'Grady's going to London tomorrow, with my father. They have a big deal to handle, and Grady has been trying to get at my father through me, though you mustn't let him know that I know. Poor dear! He's been so transparent, although he doesn't think so. We can see right through men, can't we, Amy?'

'I frequently do,' Amy replied. 'X-rays, you know.'

Tony laughed, but Julia Sandford was above that sort of thing. She kept a level gaze on Amy's face.

'I'm dropping into the hospital tomorrow to see little Jane for Grady. Someone has got to help him with that child. God knows he doesn't need problems like her around at a time like this. He's got more than enough to cope with. He gets through enough work to daunt two men.'

Grady came back with a tray, and he kept his eyes on Amy's face as he set the glasses on the table. Then he sat down, and one of his knees came into contact with Amy's thigh. He leaned across the table towards her, speaking loud to make himself heard above the general din.

'I'm sorry, Amy, about tomorrow evening, but we'll make it as soon as we can when I get this business deal concluded. I'm leaving for London in the morning.'

'With my father,' Julia Sandford said. 'He's only going along for the fun.'

'Then he'll be disappointed,' Grady said with a smile. 'We won't get any fun, unless we pull off this deal to our satisfaction.'

'How long will you be away?' Amy asked him.

'Just a couple of days. We'll stay overnight and come back the following day. I'll give you a ring as soon as I get back, or better still, I'll come along to the hospital. And you can tell Jane tomorrow that I'll bring her back a nice present. Will you do that for me?'

'Of course.' Amy nodded, a soft smile appearing on her lips.

'I'm going to drop in there tomorrow, Grady,' Julia Sandford said archly.

'Don't go and upset the child,' he warned, and Amy met his eyes across the rim of the glass. 'Some women have a way with children, and others seem to antagonise them. I know which category Amy comes under, but you're an unknown quantity, Julia.'

'That's hardly my fault,' the girl said plaintively. 'You never give me the chance to show you what I can do. Amy has an advantage over me.'

Tony caught Amy's eye. He cocked an eyebrow and glanced towards the door. Amy nodded. She finished her drink and stood up.

'We really must be leaving now,' she said.

'Must you really?' Grady got to his feet as Tony stood up. 'The evening is young yet.'

'It might be for you business types,' Amy replied with a smile, 'but if you worked in a hospital you'd soon change your habits.'

'Perhaps you're right. Take good care of Jane for me, won't you?'

'I take care of all my patients,' Amy replied.

'I'm sure you do, and I wouldn't mind being ill if I had someone like you to nurse me.' There was warmth in Grady's voice, and Amy thrilled to the expression in his blue eyes.

'You don't have far to look,' Julia Sandford said thinly.

'You don't have the necessary qualifications, Julia,' he said smilingly. 'If I was left to your tender care I should be dead within a week, I'm sure.' He took Amy's hand. 'Goodnight, my beloved doctor,' he told her.

'Goodnight, Grady.' Amy had to avert her eyes from his smiling face. 'I'll see you when you get back from London.'

'Goodnight, Gilmour, Julia,' Tony said in expressionless tones. 'Come along, Amy.' He took her arm and led her to the door, and Amy had to resist the impulse to turn and stare at Grady.

When they stepped outside into the cold night air she heaved a sigh of relief. Tony paused, glancing into her shadowed face.

'You don't have to tell me anything, Amy,' he said tightly. 'It stuck out a mile back in there. I hope Julia didn't notice your expression, but I don't think she was watching you as closely as I did.'

'Was it as bad as that, Tony?' she demanded, her heart almost missing a beat. 'You don't think Grady saw it, do you?'

'You want him to know, don't you?' he demanded slowly, without rancour. 'I'm losing you to the big man. That much I do know, but you're going to have to fight Julia for him. You know that, don't you?'

'She's making a play for him, and a big one,' Amy said, nodding her head as they walked into the car park. 'But I don't think he has any feelings for her, Tony.'

'I wish he'd fall for her and leave you to me,' he replied ruefully. He was silent until he had got into the car and leaned across to open the door for her. 'Are you sure it's Gilmour you want?'

'I've never been more sure of anything,' she told him. 'It's not just Grady, you know. There's little Jane Gilmour, too.'

'It's a big responsibility, Amy,' he said gravely, driving slowly out of the park. 'But you are a responsible person, aren't you? There's no comparison between you and Julia. I couldn't see her at home on Pent's Hill. Oh, she'd fit into the decor all right, handling the social side of it, but she's not the type to make a career out of the wife and mother business. But you would have to change your life completely, Amy. It would be goodbye to the hospital and all that.'

'I do believe you're right,' she said softly. 'But one has to make sacrifices in this world.'

'You found that out the hard way.' He glanced briefly at her. 'That's why I want you to find what you're looking for, Amy. I only hope you won't get hurt in this situation.'

'I've experienced the worst blow that can befall a human being,' she retorted. 'But I can still be hurt. I shall be careful, Tony, and I feel truly sorry for you. We've been such good friends. I hope you won't feel too badly about it. But it is better to know now than later.'

'I absolutely agree with you, although it doesn't make me any happier to know it's right.' He stared into the brilliant tunnel opened up in the night by his lights. 'I just hope that Gilmour measures up to your expectations.'

'Tony, you're talking as if he has any feelings for me,' Amy said quickly. She was afraid to bring her real feelings out into the open, because by doing so she would acknowledge the situation and admit it, thereby committing herself to her emotions. 'Anyone can see that his head is filled with nothing but business. The only reason Julia is with him now is because her influence with her father is an asset.'

'He's not all that hard-headed,' Tony replied. 'He's got one weak link in his armour, and that's his daughter. You're on the inside with her, and that means him. Don't you make any mistake about that, Amy. What other qualities Grady Gilmour might and might not have I wouldn't know, but it's plain that he's serious about being a father. If you're keen to get him then play along with the daughter. You're on a safe bet with that angle. You'll beat Julia out of sight.'

'That's a crude way of putting it,' she replied, smiling. 'But I hope you're right.'

They returned to Barnbridge and Tony drove her home. When they stopped outside the door Amy turned to him. He switched off the engine and regarded her in the faint light that came from the dashboard.

'Thank you, Tony, for everything,' she said. 'I only wish I could repay some of your kindness in the way you would wish.'

'But I know it is impossible,' he finished for her, and his teeth glinted in the semi-darkness. 'Save my blushes, Amy. I hope that big man will find the time to make you happy. But I want you to remember that I'm around. Don't forget that I'm alive, will you. If you should ever find yourself in need of anything then give me a ring. You have my number.'

She nodded as she opened the door. The cold air struck quickly, and she shivered.

'I'll see you again,' he called. 'But something tells me that much of your free time in future will be spoken for. Goodnight and good luck to you, Amy.'

She watched him drive away, and

stood for a moment straining her eyes at the empty street after he had disappeared from sight. There was deep joy inside her such as she had not experienced for a very long time. She pictured Grady's face as she had seen him in the pub, and she knew that she could ask for nothing more than his love. She turned and went into the house with her thoughts set in the future, and it was the first time for as long as she cared to remember that the nagging thoughts of her private world of grief did not intrude upon her.

Aunt Marjorie was in the kitchen, knitting a scarf for Dr Davis. She looked up with a smile as Amy opened the door, and she put aside her knitting with a sigh.

'Hello, dear,' she greeted. 'Had a nice time? Tony is such a companionable young man.'

'He is, but I'm not looking for that sort of thing,' Amy said smilingly. 'In another fifteen years perhaps I shall think differently, but not yet.'

Her aunt regarded her for a moment. Then she nodded knowingly, her blue eyes bright as a bird's. She got to her feet and went to the pantry, and her deliberate movements were made to cover her thoughts. Amy knew her aunt well enough to understand each mannerism, and she knew that something bordering a lecture would be forthcoming. She smiled. She loved Aunt Marjorie. But she decided to forestall her approach.

'Aunt,' she said. 'Do you think I should marry Tony if he asked me?'

'I certainly do, if you love him.' Her aunt turned swiftly in the doorway of the pantry, and there was a smile on her thin lips. 'Has he proposed?'

'No.' Amy shook her head and sat down at the table.

'Do you love him?' The question was as sharp as a sword thrust, and there was an intent expression upon Marjorie Davis' kind face.

'Not enough to marry him, Aunt.' Amy sighed.

'Have you got anything on your mind?' The older woman was caught up now.

'Someone else?' Amy smiled. 'That would be telling. I'm afraid you'll have to wait and watch, Aunt.'

'Just so long as you don't get hurt, dear.' There was a tinge of anxiety in the tones now, and Amy crossed to her aunt's side and put an arm around her shoulders.

'You've done more than enough worrying over me, Aunt,' she said severely. 'There's no need for any more. It's taken a long time but I think I'm fully recovered now from the tragedy. I can even think of it without inwardly cringing, so I must have made a lot of progress in the past week.'

'Another interest in life. It's as easy as that,' her aunt said wisely.

Amy had to agree. She had known the truth of it for a long time, but she had been unable to apply the knowledge where it would have done the most good. She was only human, subject to the whole gamut of hopes, fears and weaknesses that beset humans. But Time had helped her through the blackest period of her life, and Chance had brought along the fresh interest exactly when it was needed. But she knew that a setback would throw her down the slippery slope to perdition, past the low mark where she had wallowed for so long, and there would be no second ascension from the depths. The next time would be for good, and that frightened her.

She was essentially a creature of the sunlight, needing the warmth of human contact and love to sustain her, and these things she had been denied by catastrophe. But there were now two humans in her life who could become most important if they wished, and she was subconsciously hoping that they would feel the same driving force that thrust her towards them. They were magnets drawing her out of the darkness of grief, but they had the added power of being able to repel, and Amy had no desire to be spurned. She would make no overtures. If she permitted either of them to make the advances then she would not get hurt. She could only wait and hope, and it seemed to her that she had done nothing else in her lifetime . . .

7

Amy found herself unusually busy the next day, and hardly found time to think about her personal life. After her morning round, when she decided that Jane Gilmour would be fit for discharge within the week, she checked with Administration about the holidays she was due, and arranged to take a week off following Jane's discharge. She went back to the children's ward to tell Jane, and found the girl in high spirits. Amy's news made the girl positively radiant.

'And will you really come and stay with us for a whole week?' the girl demanded.

'If your father is agreeable,' Amy replied.

'He wants you to come, he told me so when I mentioned it to him. He said I could have anything I want when I get back home.'

'Did he tell you that?' Amy smiled happily. 'Then you are a very lucky girl. You must love your father very much.'

'I do. I had to make a promise to him before he would agree to your coming with us.'

'And what was that, or is it a secret?'

'I don't want any secrets from you, Doctor Amy,' the girl replied. 'I had to promise that I wouldn't do anything silly again, like running away from home to look for mummy. Daddy and I will have some fun without her. She didn't love me very much to start with because she went off and left me.'

'Did your father tell you that?'

'No. I worked it out for myself.'

Amy had to smile, but it was no laughing matter that a girl so young should have to face up to one of the hardships of life. She patted the child's shoulder.

'I've got some more news for you, Jane,' she said. 'I'm going to let you go home in a few days. Does that please you?'

'Yes, but I don't want to go until you can come. When will you start your holiday?'

'Next Monday. I thought perhaps you should go home a few days before then to help get the house ready for my visit. You want it to look at its best, don't you?'

'Of course.' The girl laughed merrily, and Amy took her leave, happy that this child's problems had faded away. She didn't think there was any chance of a recurrence of the state of mind which had led to the girl's illness.

During the afternoon she found time to revisit Jane, knowing that the girl would miss her father's visit, and she was momentarily surprised when she found Julia Sandford seated by the bed. Then she remembered the girl's words. She had mentioned that she planned to visit Jane. There was calculation in that move, Amy could tell, and she remained in the background, watching the girl's attempts to make friends with Jane. Apparently she was trying in vain, judging by Jane's expression, and Amy turned and departed before she was seen.

Just before she went off duty for the evening she dropped back into the children's ward to say goodbye to Jane, and when she paused by the girl's bed Jane burst into tears. Amy frowned as she sat down quickly. She took the girl's hand, speaking in soothing tones.

'What's the matter, Jane? Are you missing your father today? Never mind, he'll be back tomorrow, and I'll bet that he'll make this place his first call. I'll stay with you a little while if you like. But you should be thinking about next week. We're going to have a lot of fun together.'

'It isn't Daddy I'm thinking about,' the girl retorted, drying her eyes. 'It was Julia Sandford. I don't like her. She came to see me this afternoon. All she did was ask me questions about Daddy. I'm only a child, but I knew what she was hinting at. She wants to marry Daddy.'

'Did she tell you that?' Amy demanded.

'She didn't have to say it. She asked a lot of silly questions. She wanted to know if I'd ever thought about having another mother. I told her I had — you!'

'And what did she say to that?'

'She didn't like it. She said we would be happy together, but I don't like her, Doctor Amy. She's coming back this evening to bring me a present, she said, but I don't want to see her.'

Amy patted the girl's shoulder. So Julia couldn't wait to start her ensnaring, and she was making a firm footing for herself with Jane, or so she thought. Amy listened to the girl sniffing, and shook her head.

'I'll tell Julia not to visit you this evening,' she said. 'Don't worry about her, Jane. Your father will be back tomorrow. He'll come and see you and you can talk to him.'

'I wish you would stay with us at Pent's Hill,' the girl retorted. 'It's such a frightening house. I never have any friends up there. Daddy is always out, and there are just the servants.'

'Never mind. I told you things would be different when you went back home, and they will be. Don't worry about anything, Jane. Just you wait and see.'

'I wouldn't mind Daddy marrying again if he married you. But I wouldn't want Julia for my next mother.'

'I have a feeling that you don't have to worry about that, Jane, although I shouldn't say so. You just wait and see. If you wish hard enough for something then the magic starts working, and you'll find everything coming right.'

The girl lay down, and Amy took her leave. On her way out she saw Sister Lockwood, and they spoke for several minutes. The Sister had something to say about Julia Sandford.

'Flighty, she is, and too full of herself. She upset little Jane by coming to see her.'

'I'm going to ring her now,' Amy said. 'She intends coming back this evening with a present.'

'You'd better do that, and tell her that another visit wouldn't be in the best interests of the patient.'

'I'll use your office if I may.'

'With pleasure.' Sister Lockwood opened the door and held it open for Amy to enter. She closed it behind Amy before going into the ward, and Amy went to the desk and reached for the telephone.

She knew enough of Julia Sandford's character to know that she would be stirring up trouble for herself by interfering, as Julia would regard it. Julia would immediately think that Amy was planning something in the nature of her own plans, and Amy tightened her lips as she flicked through the directory and found the Sandford number. She hesitated before ringing, then steeled herself for an ordeal. She took a deep breath as she dialled the number.

A maid answered the phone, and Amy gave her name with misgiving. But she had Jane to think of, she told herself. The child was progressing nicely, and any set-back now would be too great for the girl's new-found confidence.

'Hello!' Julia's voice carried a faint trace of condescension, and Amy recalled that the same manner had been apparent the night before at the table in the little pub.

'This is Doctor Merrill,' she said formally. 'I'm afraid that your visit this afternoon was not a success, Julia. Jane is upset, and I wouldn't advise your return this evening.'

'Upset!' Julia echoed. There was a pause while she took it in. 'Why, the little fool! She didn't have to take it all literally. What can be done with a child like that?' There was a heavy sigh of exasperation. 'Are you ordering me to stay away this evening?'

'Certainly not. In the interests of my patient I'm asking you to stay away.'

'I see.' There was an unmistakable sneer in the soft tones. 'So Jane told you what I'd been saying to her this afternoon, did she? And you didn't like it at all! You've got some plans of your own, Doctor Merrill, I can see, but I'm telling you that it's no use. I'm going to marry Grady Gilmour.'

'If you do then I'll wish you both very good luck,' Amy said. Her fingers tightened around the receiver. She could imagine the girl's face and expression at the other end of the line. 'My only interest is the patient's welfare.'

'I think you're taking too much on yourself. I shall tell Grady about this. Just because he's taken you out once you're getting big ideas. Well you're wasting your time, Doctor. It won't help you in the least to get in with Grady's daughter. If he marries me she'll go to a boarding school.'

'Will you stay away from Jane this evening?' Amy demanded.

'Of course I will. I wouldn't worry if I never saw the little brat again.'

'Thank you. Goodnight.' Amy hung up, cutting off the flow of angry chatter.

She was trembling as she left the office, and she paused for a moment outside the ward to compose herself before entering to go to Jane's bedside.

'Did you speak to her?' the girl demanded.

'Yes.' Amy nodded, smiling now. 'She won't be coming to see you. Now you just settle down, and in the morning I expect your father will telephone me and ask how you are.'

'Ask him when he'll be coming in tomorrow,' Jane said.

'I'll do that.' Amy straightened the covers automatically. She bent and impulsively kissed the girl's cheek. 'I'm going off duty now, Jane,' she whispered. 'I've had a tiring day. You'll be good to the nurses, won't you?'

'I'll do anything you say,' the child told her. 'See you in the morning.'

Amy left with a warm feeling spreading through her breast. She drove slowly home, thinking about the child's future. What would happen to Jane if Grady did marry Julia? She shuddered to think of it. But she knew now that Julia was serious in her attempts to win Grady for herself. Julia had a reputation of getting what she wanted. But this time she had to fail, and Amy was not thinking of herself, of her own future, when she decided it. Jane's future was what counted, and if it meant trying to attract Grady herself then she would do it to prevent Julia accomplishing what she intended.

She smiled at the thought. A few weeks ago her mind would have been too busy dwelling in the past, and she would have been horrified by any suggestion from within that she should deliberately attempt to vamp a man, especially someone like Grady Gilmour. She was sincerely in love with him, but desperation was needling her now, and she knew she was capable of anything. All the love that she had felt for her own dead daughter seemed to pour towards the motherless Jane Gilmour.

She was in a turmoil when she went into the house, but sight of Aunt

Marjorie steadied her.

'Late again!' Marjorie Davis studied Amy's face for signs of how her niece's day had gone. 'Have you been working too hard again?'

'Does it show?' Amy smiled. 'But it's not the work that worries me, Aunt. There's a complication arisen in Jane Gilmour's life, and it affects me.'

'She's not had a relapse!'

'Nothing like that. Julia Sandford was in to see her today because Grady is in London. When I saw Jane after Julia's visit the poor child was crying. Julia intends marrying Grady, and she's decided that the quickest way to his heart is through Jane, but she said all the wrong things.'

'That's typical of Julia Sandford,' her aunt remarked.

'Jane is making nice progress, mentally, I mean. We had fears for her when she was first admitted, but I've managed to gain her confidence, and now she would do anything for me. By the way, Aunt, I'm taking a week's holiday next week and I'm going to the Gilmour house on Pent's Hill to spend the time with Jane.'

'Is that wise?' There was no reproach in Marjorie Davis' voice.

'I don't know. I'm only thinking of my patient. Returning to that big house alone might retard her complete recovery. I'm not talking about her illness. That is cleared up now. Drugs can take care of that kind of trouble, but the mind is another matter.'

'I know exactly how you're thinking, Amy. I think you should do what you can for this child, but at the same time you must know that you can go too far. You're in love with Grady Gilmour, and that's a good thing. You deserve to find some happiness in this world. But if Julia Sandford has her eyes on him then you'd better not take any chances, because she won't overlook anything in her fight to get him.'

'I think I have Julia's measure, Aunt.' Amy spoke softly. 'I could see the other evening that Grady was not attracted to her. He's been seeing her lately because he wanted to push through a business deal in which her father figures prominently. This trip to London he's making now is the culmination of his efforts, and if it goes through successfully then Julia Sandford will find out exactly where she stands.'

'I hope it works out that way for you,' Marjorie Davis said, shaking her head. 'But you'd better be prepared for disappointment, Amy. You know better than most how upsets can come along. I think you've had more than your share in the past, but Life has a habit of slapping down the more unfortunates time after time.'

Amy silently agreed with her aunt, and she was thoughtful as she ate her tea. There was so much that could go wrong, but she was not worried for herself. She didn't want to see Jane Gilmour getting hurt and, as far as the child went, her mind was geared for war with Julia Sandford. But she realized that Grady held all the important answers. If he fell in love with Julia then no amount of action would prevent disaster for the child. Amy didn't think he was in the least attracted to Julia, but one could never tell.

She spent the evening catching up on some household chores that she had neglected, but her mind was not on her work. She was wondering how Grady was making out in London. The evening seemed to drag, and she was relieved when it was time to go to bed. Sleep was a blessing when it came, for it obliterated all the nagging thoughts and the restlessness.

Next morning she was awake early, and found her aunt in the kitchen preparing breakfast. The older woman glanced at the clock on the wall, and Amy smiled.

'Yes,' she said. 'My mind wouldn't let me rest. But today might see the clearing up of some problems. I'm sure Julia will try to score off me. She's bound to mention my call to her. She'll do anything to discredit me in Grady's eyes.'

'If he's the man I think he is then he won't be taken in by Julia Sandford. You did what was right for your patient, and he'll be quick to see that. You tell me he's got the child's welfare at heart after having neglected her. Well that kind of a change in a man is sweeping. I don't think you have any cause to worry, Amy.'

Amy hopefully agreed, but she was deeply worried when she set out for the hospital. She arrived earlier than usual, and was quite impatient for the day's routine to start. The morning passed slowly, and she realized that she was waiting for the telephone to ring, hoping to hear Grady's voice on the line, and each time a call came through her heart leaped like a fractious dog and she felt choked with unaccustomed emotion. But there was no call from him, and in her heart she knew he would not reach Barnbridge before noon. The only bright spot in her morning was when she visited Jane in the children's ward.

'Hello, Doctor Amy,' the child greeted her, and Amy's worries fled before the sight of this happy child.

'How are you feeling this morning, Jane?'

'Much better, thank you. Has Daddy telephoned yet?'

'No, dear. But he won't be back before lunch. Perhaps he will arrange it so he's here this afternoon to visit you.'

'I hope Julia won't come again. I couldn't sleep very well last night, thinking about what she said.'

'I don't think she will. I spoke to her last night and she understands.'

'I can't wait for next week to come,' the child said. 'What shall we do, Doctor Amy? Will you stay with us night and day, or shall you go home every evening?'

'I'm not sure. We'd better leave it to your father to make the arrangements. He is the boss, you know.'

'He told me that I'm the boss now,' the girl said proudly.

'And I'm sure he means it. He'll be

very pleased to see how well you've got on.'

'He promised to buy me a present before he comes back. I hope he won't forget. I'm looking forward to it.'

'He won't forget. Your father isn't like that.'

'He used to be. But he was always worried about business. There were more important things on his mind. But since I've been ill, he says, he's found out which is more important, and that's me.'

Amy smiled as she patted the child's shoulder. She went on with her routine, uplifted by the knowledge that everything was coming right for the girl. She returned to her office just before noon, and had barely sat down at her desk when the telephone rang. She grabbed up the receiver, and the next instant Grady's voice was in her ear.

'Hello, Amy, how's everything at the hospital?' he greeted.

'Grady, are you back in Barnbridge?'

'Yes. Just got back to the office, and

the first thing I did was ring you. How is Jane?'

'Fine. She'll be able to go home in a few days. Are you coming in to see her this afternoon?'

'Of course. She's my favourite girl.' He seemed bubbling over with good humour.

'Did you get the present you promised her?' Amy demanded.

'Good Lord no!' He tut-tutted. 'I completely forgot it. It's a good thing you're around. I'll nip into a store this afternoon on my way to see her and get something. What would she like, do you think?'

'Grady, you should know your own child. I don't know what's she's already got. You may be the kind of father who doesn't make a habit of buying presents.'

'The way I forgot to get this one shows that I haven't had much practice at it,' he responded, laughing. 'But I'll make up for it. I'm bound to find it difficult, becoming the perfect father.

But everything gets easier with practice. Just give me a little time.'

'You've got all the time in the world now,' Amy said happily. 'I'm greatly relieved to report that Jane is looking forward to returning home. But there is something I should like to talk over with you before you see Jane. Will you call at my office before going into the ward this afternoon?'

'With pleasure. Say two-thirty?'

'I'll be here,' she said.

'Good. Now I must ring off. I've got some work to do. Everything went well for me in London. I expect to be a millionaire by the time I'm forty-five.'

'Congratulations.' Amy smiled as she hung up. Relief was bubbling up inside her. Was she worrying unnecessarily? She had spent so many months with grief in her heart and mind that the feeling of complete easiness left her wondering what was wrong. Everything gets easier with practice! She thought of Grady's words. She needed to get in a lot of practice with just ordinary emotions, and she had made a good start with Jane.

On her way to lunch she walked into the children's ward to tell Jane that her father had telephoned, and it gave her great pleasure to see the happiness which spread over the child's face.

'Did he say anything about a present?' Jane demanded.

'He did mention something about it, but he asked me not to tell you, so don't let it out, will you.'

'What is it?'

'I don't know. You'll have to wait until he comes in.'

'I always seem to be waiting for the good things,' the child complained. 'Is it ever any different in life?'

'I don't think it is, and as you get older, Jane, you'll find that half the pleasure in the good things is the anticipation. Now you rest up for this afternoon, and I shall be along to see you after your father has gone.'

Amy found that she was becoming impatient as two-thirty came nearer.

There was a fluttering in her breast and her pulses were behaving erratically. She was behind her desk well before the half-hour, and when there was a heavy knock on the door she fairly flew out of the seat to answer it. Opening the door, she found Grady standing there. He was holding a long box under one arm, and there was a bunch of carefully wrapped carnations stuck under the other elbow. He was smiling widely, and seemed in high spirits.

'Hello, Amy,' he greeted, coming forward quickly to enter the room. He thrust the flowers at her with a flourish. 'Good thing it's a hospital you work in or I'd look out of place carrying a bunch of flowers.'

'Are they for me?' she demanded with great pleasure.

'Unless you think Jane would like the flowers and you'd rather have this doll.' He grinned as he laid the long box on the desk.

'Thanks. I think I'll keep the flowers. They're beautiful, Grady.'

'Just a small mark of my gratitude,' he replied. 'You've done a lot for Jane, and that means me. I'm feeling like the happiest man in the world, and I can tell you that I haven't felt like this for a very long time. It's all due to you, Amy. I think you're an angel in disguise. Before we get down to business I want to tell you that we're going out tonight.' He paused, still grinning. 'That's if you can make it. Are you free?'

'I am,' Amy replied. 'But won't you be seeing Julia?'

'Julia.' His face hardened momentarily. 'Let's talk about Julia for a moment, shall we?' He drew a quick breath. 'She was ringing my office every half-hour this morning, from ten until I got in, and she was bursting with indignation about the way you treated her. You refused to let her see Jane last night.'

'Did she say that?' Amy smiled. 'I rang her and suggested that it would be better for Jane if she didn't call.'

'She came in yesterday afternoon,'

Grady said. 'What happened to upset Jane?'

'It's none of my business, Grady.'

'I can ask Jane, but that might upset her. I don't want to do that. You've done a grand job on her, and nothing must upset her, nothing. But you don't have to say anything, Amy. I know Julia quite well by now. I suffered enough in her company while I was trying to put this deal through, but thank God that's over and done with. I can imagine some of the things she said to Jane. No doubt Jane will mention it to me this afternoon. Was there something on your mind? You said you wanted to see me before I saw Jane. Was it about Julia?'

'No. It's about Jane. She'll be going home in a day or two, and I've promised to spend some time with her. I'm taking a week's holiday next week, and she's quite looking forward to being with me.'

'And you're quite happy to spend a week's holiday with her?' Grady shook his head. 'Jane is luckier than she knows. What plans have you made?'

'None at all. I decided to wait and get your blessing first. You're her father.'

'So I do get some say in this matter!' He was smiling again. 'Well, I've got news for you, Doctor Amy. I've been making a few plans myself. As I told you, nothing matters now except Jane and her welfare. So if you can give up a week's holiday for my child then so can I. I'm going to take a week off next week, like you, and if you'll let me come along with you and Jane I promise not to get in the way or give you any trouble.'

There was a little-boy expression on his face, and his blue eyes were glinting. Amy felt her heart swell with emotion, and happiness bubbled inside her.

'Won't you find it terribly dull?' she demanded. She was standing beside her desk, and he was a couple of feet away, one hand on the desk, his weight resting upon it. He was smiling, and he reached out a big hand and his fingers dug into her shoulder.

'I shall be extremely happy,' he told her. 'You see, Amy, I'm in love with you.'

8

His casual statement took Amy completely by surprise. She gasped, and he laughed huskily, his fingers tightening their grip upon her shoulder. He straightened as he drew her towards him, and there was an intentness in his expression that communicated with something in her soul. She knew what he was going to do, but she was powerless to think or act. He slid his arms around her and she was crushed against his chest. His arms were hard about her slim shoulders.

'I don't care if this little act ruins a very promising friendship,' he said softly.

Before she could make reply his mouth was down against hers, and Amy felt a swift surge of emotions. She was overwhelmed by her feelings, and although her instincts were to resist she could not find the necessary strength. She closed her eyes, and seemed to sink beneath the surface of a warm sea of love. There was a buzzing sound in her ears, and she was stirred deeply. For a week she had been conscious of restlessness, an uneasy feeling of attraction and love for this man. She had imagined herself to be in love with him, and yet she had been afraid that loneliness had been the spur. But his lips against her mouth proved beyond all reasonable doubt that she was in love with him. And he had just confessed his love for her.

When he was breathless he released her, but maintained his embrace, staring down into her face with his sparkling blue eyes. There was tenderness in his expression, and he smiled.

'Amy, have I ruined our friendship?' he demanded huskily. 'I know I shouldn't have handled it like this, but today I'm on top of the world. I love you, and I'm prepared to wait for you to get used to the idea. Don't tell me that I've made a fool of myself.'

'I couldn't tell you that,' she replied softly. She was aware that her cheeks were hot, and knew she must be blushing like a schoolgirl. She was breathing deeply, and her blood was pounding through her temples. 'I've known for a week that I'm in love with you.'

'Really?' There was such wonder and hope in his eyes. He pulled her into his embrace more tightly, but she struggled this time.

'Please, Grady,' she said urgently. 'Someone might come in, and I'd never be able to explain this.'

'All right. But we're going out this evening, remember. I can't really believe that this is true. When I saw you out with Tony Walker the other evening I thought I had come too late upon the scene.'

'Tony is just a good friend.'

'But he's in love with you. That much I saw in him.'

'Tony knows there's no hope for him. I told him as much.'

'Then there's nothing to stop us from

getting together.' The eagerness in his voice sent thrills through Amy's breast. 'I could hardly force myself to go to London, knowing that I loved you,' Grady went on. 'Nothing matters now. Once my business was everything, but it's taking a real back seat. You get along well with Jane, don't you, Amy? It's important that you do. I want to do what is right for her. I knew as soon as she met Julia that there could be nothing doing. Right from the start Julia was flogging a dead horse as far as I was concerned. But apart from Jane's point of view, Julia wasn't the kind of girl I could love.'

'You didn't string her along just for the sake of a business partnership, did you?'

'No. It wasn't like that. I used to see a lot of her father, and you know Julia. She's after every unattached man in sight.'

'And you wouldn't profess to love a woman just because she happened to get along well with your daughter, would you?'

'Of course not.' He smiled easily and

put his arms around her. 'That first time I saw you in the waiting room, when Jane was just getting through the crisis of her illness, I thought that I have never seen a more eligible woman. I'm something of a perfectionist, I warn you, and you matched up to every ideal.'

'That must be a tall order. I'll take it as a compliment.' Amy moved away from him, going around the desk to sit down. She looked up at him. His face was a picture of happiness. 'Now you'd better go and see Jane. She's beside herself with impatience.'

'I'll go right away.' He picked up the long box containing the doll. 'I'll see you this evening, Amy?'

'Whenever you want,' she told him.

'Seven-thirty. I'll be through at the office by then. I have to arrange for next week. Shall we go away, or would you prefer to stay around Barnbridge?'

'I think we'd better leave it up to Jane. She must figure largely in everything, and be given the opportunity of helping make the plans.'

174

'Of course. You're so right, Amy. Now I had better be going. I'll see you this evening at seven-thirty.'

After he had gone Amy sat stiff and frozen, her mind clicking over what had ensued. The thought that hammered through her mind was just like a pulse gone berserk. Grady loved her! Her own feelings had been intensified by his declaration. Now there was no hope for her. She was well and truly in love, and that was something she thought could never happen again in her life. Dare she close her eyes to the past and look into the future? Could she hope that one day Grady would ask her to be his wife, to act as a mother to his daughter? There was an ache deep in Amy's heart. She was filled with intense longing for some close human contact. Grady Gilmour, she thought. Jane Gilmour. Already they were beginning to fill her world.

The rest of the afternoon seemed unreal. Amy went through the motions of her routine as if in a dream. There seemed to be ethereal voices singing in her mind, raising ghostly voices in ecstasy. She felt exalted, beyond the ordinary day, the general atmosphere of the hospital, and she wished that she would never lose the feeling. Happiness had returned to her, and she intended clutching at it with both hands.

Later she called in to see Jane, and found the girl sitting up in bed clasping the doll Grady had bought for her. She looked at Amy with happiness in her blue eyes.

'Look at this beautiful doll,' she cried. 'I'm calling her Doctor Amy. Do you mind?'

'Not in the least. I think it's a good name for a doll. How did you find your father, Jane?'

'He's so different, Doctor Amy. That business deal in London must have gone off well.'

'I'm sure it did. Would you like me to make some clothes for Doctor Amy? She must have a nightdress and a swim suit. She'll need an evening dress and some warm clothes for the winter.'

'Can we wait until next week and do them together?'

'Of course. I shall need some help.' Amy's voice softened. 'It's been such a long time since I had to make doll's clothes.' For a moment there was a picture in her mind, showing two faces; that of her dead husband and the never-to-be-forgotten features of her lost child. But there was no attendant pain now. The heartache was fading. The past was settling down where it belonged. Her mind had been oppressed far too long. Now it had thrown off the bitter yoke of the past three years. Soon she would be able to look back without emotion.

'I told Daddy about next week, and he's going to take off the time to be with us. He's told me to think about what we should do and where we should go. I don't have to do anything I won't like, and you'll go wherever I say.'

'Yes. It will be your week, Jane, and whatever you wish shall be done.'

'You're going to stay at Pent's Hill with us?'

'If you want. You have only to say.'

'Do you like me, Doctor Amy?'

'Very much, Jane. I had an empty place in my heart and you came along and filled it.'

'I missed my Mummy. That's why I ran away and got ill, but since I've been here I don't miss her any more. I like you as much as I ever liked her.'

Amy patted her shoulder, unable to speak for the moment. A child's love so freely given was the most precious gift in the world, she thought. To have it and hold it was important to the child.

'I'm sure we're going to get along very well together, Jane.'

'Daddy said he wouldn't be bringing Julia to the house any more. I didn't like her, Doctor Amy. She asked so many questions. I think she wants to marry Daddy.'

'You don't have to worry about that, dear. Your Daddy has no interest in her.'

'He said he likes you. I'm glad. I like you. Wouldn't it be nice if Daddy married you? Then you wouldn't come to Pent's Hill just for next week. You could stay all the time.'

'You mustn't worry your head about things like that, Jane,' Amy told her. 'I'm sure everything will work out right for you in the end.'

The girl turned happily to her doll, and Amy took her leave, glancing anxiously at her watch. She didn't want to keep Grady waiting when he called for her. She hurried back to her office to tidy up for the day, and then she went home.

At seven-thirty she was ready, standing by the window in the sitting room, watching for Grady's arrival. Aunt Marjorie had made some small attempt at conversation during tea, but after realizing that Amy had something on her mind, and was also brimming over with inner happiness, the older woman wisely kept silent. She didn't need to be told what was in the air, and she was very happy.

Grady arrived and stepped out of his

big car. He saw her at the window, and waved. Aunt Marjorie opened the door to him, and Amy hurried into the hall to find them talking together.

'Have a nice time,' Aunt Marjorie called as they left the house.

'Where would you like to go?' Grady asked as he helped her into the car. 'I don't like the idea of taking you into a pub.'

'I thought you would have all your plans made,' Amy replied with a smile.

'I did have an idea that we might make it a formal evening, but it didn't appeal to me, and I'm sure you don't feel like that after your day in the hospital. Let's just go for a drive, and perhaps we can find somewhere quiet where we can sit and talk. I've got a lot to say to you, and I'm sure you're bursting to talk about Jane.'

He went around the car and climbed in beside her. Starting the car, he glanced sideways, grinning at her.

'I've been unable to concentrate on anything in the office after seeing you this afternoon,' he said. 'I shall need that week's holiday to recover from the shock.'

'It is a shock, waking up one day and finding yourself in love,' Amy responded.

'Do you love me?' he questioned. 'Can you look me in the eyes here in the cold evening light and tell me that you do care?'

'I can and I will,' Amy said slowly, facing him. There was a small smile on her lips, and he was grinning, leaning forward intently to catch her expression. 'I love you, Grady.'

'I love you, Beloved Doctor,' he retorted, and bent forward and kissed her quickly. 'It hit me several days back. I'd been busy at the office, and when I threw down the pen to relax for a few moments a picture of your face appeared before me, just like a ghost. I felt love hit me just like that. I'm in love with Doctor Amy Merrill, I said, just like that.' He sighed. 'I thought I was having my usual bad luck when I saw you with Tony Walker, and when I found out that there was nothing serious between you I determined to plunge in, for better or worse. I had a feeling that you were attracted to me. I noticed a great change in your manner the second time I met you. Amy, I shan't ever do anything to hurt you or make you sorry that you met me.'

He drove away from the kerb before she replied, and Amy was aware of the eagerness inside her. She was breathing quickly, as if she had been running. A small voice inside her was telling her insistently that it could not be true, but she knew that it was. Grady Gilmour loved her! It had been too much to hope for, that the father of that young child could fall in love with her. At first she had wanted to love the child, and could have asked for no more than that after her three years of loneliness, but now she wanted the father too, and there was nothing to stop her getting both.

'Grady,' she said suddenly, 'we ought to discuss Jane. I don't think it right that she should be alone in that big house of yours. I know the servants are there and she is very well cared for, but it isn't the thing. She's a sensitive child, and your broken marriage affected her far more than you realized.'

'I know that, and I'm willing to do anything to put matters right,' he said. 'Tell me what I should do for the best and it will be done.'

'You've been having her educated privately, haven't you?'

'Yes. A governess used to live in. There's been a succession of them in the past few years.'

'Until Jane is older I think she should go out to school. There is a private school in the town. She ought to mix with other children.'

'Good. We'll see about that as soon as she's well enough to return to lessons. That's what I like you about you, Amy. You have everything at your fingertips. You're so damned efficient in everything that I feel awed at times.'

'Nonsense! It's just commonsense,' she returned.

'I'm going to use some commonsense for a change,' he went on. 'The business takes second place in my life. Home comes first! Home and child and you, Amy.' He glanced sideways at her. 'Am I going too fast for you? I told you this afternoon that I loved you. I think you'd better know the rest of it. I want to marry you, Amy. Would you consider a proposal?'

She was silent for a long time, and he did not interrupt her thoughts. Amy couldn't think straight. Her emotions were mixed up.

'There's a lot to be said for that stock reply,' she said at length. 'This is so sudden! I can't collect my thoughts.'

'I know, and I'm a fool for trying to rush things, but we are not youngsters in our teens or early twenties. We've missed a lot of time, Amy. I'm not going to rush you though. I haven't proposed. All I've done is told you what's in my mind. Now you know what I'm thinking and what I want ultimately. You have all the time in the world to think it over. You may think I'm not entirely sure about myself. We haven't known each other long, but I knew in the first minute that you were the girl who came closest to the picture in my mind. Love doesn't need half a lifetime to bloom, does it?'

'It doesn't,' she agreed. 'I couldn't love you more than I do, Grady. I know that as definitely as black and white are opposites. But there are so many things to be considered. I'm not a secretary who can give up a job like that for matrimony. I have to make a decision about that side of my life.'

'Amy, you don't have to give up anything that you don't want,' he said warmly. 'Stay a doctor if you like. Just so long as I get to see you sometimes I don't care. I know Jane would like to have you for a mother. We'd have no problems there. I'm not going to let the business run my life any more. If it gets too much then I'll sell out. Life is short, and we have to make the best of what we've got. I'd go out labouring for twelve pounds a week for you. We could have a wonderful life together. I'm sure you must be very lonely. I know that I am, and so is Jane. The three of us would benefit that much from our marriage, without going any farther. But with your love behind me there would be no limit to what we could achieve.'

His intense tones struck a chord in Amy's heart. She knew that he spoke the truth. Each of them had nothing to lose, but the decision was not an easy one to make. For herself, there was a shrine in her heart that had no right to be there. It was right that she should remember her previous family, and the circumstances that took them away from her, but if she remarried then her next husband, and his child, should have her undivided love and attention. Could she disassociate herself from the past to live up to the new responsibilities? The whole question would require a deal of consideration.

'Grady,' she said slowly. 'We mustn't

lose our heads and rush into this.'

'I'm not asking you to, Amy,' he replied quickly. 'Take all the time you need to think it over. For myself, I've got nothing to consider. I'm in love with you and that's good enough for me. But I can understand your situation. You'll need time to think, and that's what I'm going to give you. I'm not going to exert any pressure. All I wanted to do was let you know what was in my mind, and I've done that.'

'You certainly have,' she replied. 'I don't know if I'm on my head or my heels, Grady.'

He laughed happily and sent the powerful car forward into the night. Amy leaned back in her seat and stared ahead, trying to recover her thoughts, her sanity and her wits. Grady had tossed a bombshell at her, and she could not think clearly. In the morning, she thought, when the shock and excitement had died down a little, she would be able to give some consideration to the situation. Then there was her holiday next week, and she would spend it in their company. She would work it out, although her heart was already clamouring to be heard. But she could not let her heart rule her. She knew now what she wanted to do. It was painted in her mind in red letters a mile high. But sanity had to prevail, and she would need time to think.

'This has been quite a day, Amy,' Grady said. 'I could not get back from London quick enough to see you. On the way back I kept thinking crazy things, like Tony Walker had asked you to marry him last night and you had accepted. That's the kind of luck I've come to accept, but you've knocked the bottom out of that particular barrel. I'll never argue about my luck after this.'

She listened to his happy voice, and there was happiness in her heart. In such a short time her whole outlook had changed. Only yesterday she was aware of her love for this kind man, and now the miracle had happened and he was in love with her. He had declared his intentions, and if she wanted she could be his wife. Again she thought of her dead husband. She had remained true to his memory, but he would not have wanted her to mourn for the rest of her life. He would have wanted her to find what happiness she could. Jane could never completely replace Susan in her heart, but most of that aching void would be refilled by the child's love and affection.

Grady drove on and on through the night. He was filled with the same restlessness that gripped Amy. They had both suffered through circumstances beyond their control, and they both wanted to find a little happiness, some relief from their loneliness. They both deserved it, she knew, and she tried to put some order into her mind. She could not make any decision right now, but she knew in the back of her mind that she would never refuse his proposal. That was still in the future, and she could try to work out this and that until he asked her to marry. Then would come the difficult time. Then she would have to make her decision.

Later Grady parked, and Amy had no idea of the time, or wanted to know. They sat in the darkness in some strange lane, and Grady put his arms around her and his mouth against hers. Lost in the bliss of their contact, Amy knew she had no problems. She was lost under the barrage of wild emotions that welled up from deep inside, emotions which had been kept prisoner for so long. There was relief inside her because her bondage to grief was over. She felt as if she were reborn. She had come through the fire to find love again, and she desperately wanted to take what was being offered, to snatch the happiness she so badly needed.

They were silent in the car, aware only of each other, and Grady was gentle, tender, trying to offer her his love in a way that showed how much he respected her past. He was placing her upon a pedestal, but that was not what she wanted. She had suffered enough to know that life was for living while there was time. Nothing should be left to chance.

'Grady,' she whispered in his ear. 'This is like stepping out of the shadows again.'

'I know exactly what you mean,' he said huskily. 'I've got the same feeling. The past is a nightmare, and we're just waking up from it. Don't worry about the future, Amy. I'll see to it that nothing goes wrong.'

When she glanced at her watch she was astounded to find that midnight was almost upon them.

'Grady!' she gasped. 'The time! It's ten to twelve. I shall never be up in time for work tomorrow.'

'I'll bet you're never late on duty,' he retorted, sliding behind the wheel. 'We've got a long way to go, but don't worry. A late night now and again won't hurt you, and next week we're both free of the demands of society. What a week that will be!'

He started the engine and turned the

car, and they went speeding back towards Barnbridge. Amy sat snuggled down in the deep seat, watching the road ahead through half-closed eyes. It was all like a dream, she thought, and hoped that she would never have to wake up.

Grady turned to her when he stopped outside the house, and once more took her into his arms. Now her mind was beginning to accept that this was no dream, and when she went into the darkened house she felt like singing.

9

The next two days passed quickly, and Amy changed completely inside. The tiny frown lines above her dark eyes just vanished, and time had no meaning. Jane Gilmour went home on Thursday, and Amy had to promise to call at Pent's Hill that evening to see the child. Grady collected his daughter, promising to call for Amy that evening at his usual time. Amy walked out to the car park with them, and she wrapped a rug around the girl's knees.

'Now, Jane,' she said. 'Don't go out without a coat on, and don't sit in the draughts.'

'Don't worry, Doctor Amy,' the child replied. 'I want to be well for next week.'

Amy met Grady's gaze across the top of the girl's head, and they smiled.

'Next week will soon be here,' Grady

said. 'I'm looking forward to it as much as you, Jane, and I'm sure Doctor Amy is getting excited about it.'

'I am. It's a long time since I had a holiday.' Amy smiled down into the girl's uplifted face. 'And I couldn't spend this one with two nicer people.'

She stepped back and shut the door, and Grady waved as he drove away. When the car had departed Amy turned and walked back into the hospital, and it seemed to her that part of her heart had gone in the car.

She was impatient to see how Jane settled down at home, and the afternoon seemed long without Grady's visit, but work kept her busy, and when it was time for her to go off duty she was almost exhausted. She hurried home to prepare for the evening, and hardly touched her tea. Aunt Marjorie knew the signs well, and refrained from commenting upon the situation. Time would sort it all out. Amy was ready and waiting when Grady called for her.

Out at Pent's Mill the big house

seemed more friendly as they drove along the drive. There were lights in several of the windows, and when Grady escorted her through the big front doorway Jane came running out of the library to greet her. Amy put an arm around the girl's shoulder, feeling her instincts intensifying as she listened to the girl's happy chatter. Grady led them into the library and closed the door. The evening outside was cold, blustery, and there was a hint of rain.

'Have you decided yet what you want to do next week, Jane?' Grady asked. 'Now is the time to make your plans. Amy will want to know what's on your mind, and perhaps there are things that she won't like seeing or doing.'

'I don't know yet,' the child replied, sitting on a long sofa beside Amy, pushing long fingers into Amy's hand. 'Can we go to London for a few days?'

Grady cocked an enquiring eyebrow at Amy, who nodded.

'I think that's a good idea,' she said. 'I haven't been to London in years, and there must be a lot of new things to see.'

'London it is,' Grady said firmly. 'When shall we leave?'

'Monday morning,' Jane said.

'All right. Now I suggest that you go up to bed, young lady. You're not quite well yet, and you mustn't overtax yourself.' Grady got to his feet and took Jane's hand, but the girl pulled away.

'We haven't shown Doctor Amy the room she'll have when she stays here. Can I take her up now?'

'Of course.' Grady smiled goodnaturedly. 'But if we're going to London then our beloved doctor won't be able to stay here.'

'We're not going for the whole week,' the child said happily. 'We'll come back after two days.' She stood up and tugged at Amy's hand. 'Come along and I'll show you the room I've picked out for you. It's next to mine.'

Amy spent a happy half-hour with Jane, then persuaded the child to go to bed. She helped change the girl's clothes for a nightdress, then took her down to the library to say goodnight to her father. Grady seemed pleased to see them taking to each other, and Amy was happy when she took Jane up to bed. The girl held up her face to be kissed, and Amy hugged her for a moment.

'Goodnight, Jane,' she whispered. 'I'm so happy that you have settled down here again.'

'Only because you've come to see me,' the child whispered. 'You won't ever leave us now, will you, Doctor Amy?'

'Not as long as you need me, dear,' Amy replied, and it was a cry from her heart.

When she went down to the library again she found Grady standing before the fire, a glass of whisky in one hand, and there was a tight smile on his lips. He held out a hand to her when she appeared in the doorway, and Amy went to him, standing close to him by the fire.

'It did me good to see you two together,' he said slowly. 'I can see now what that child has been missing. I've been a fool, Amy. I almost ruined Jane's life because of my ignorance.'

'It's all right now,' she replied. 'Jane is very happy again.'

'No thanks to me,' he said bitterly. 'You're an angel. Whatever should I have done if I'd never met you?'

'You would have found a solution,' she replied. 'You're an intelligent man, kind and compassionate. You would eventually have realized what was wrong with Jane, and you would have put it right.'

He set down his glass and put his arms around her. Amy looked up into his strong face, and she saw the love and hope in his features. His blue eyes were alight with emotion, and she pressed her head against his shoulder.

'I love you, Amy. I never thought I should love another woman, but here I am telling you, and it's the most wonderful feeling in the world. I'm a lucky man. There's no doubt about that. All I hope is that everything will work out right for the both of us.'

'Is there any reason why it shouldn't?' She raised her head and looked up at him.

'No.' He shook his head, tightening his grip about her. 'You mean Marion, don't you? My divorce came through a long time ago. She remarried quickly. She's living up in Scotland now.' He smiled down at her. 'There are no other complications. I have to prove my love for you, and that's all. If you find you love me enough to marry me then I'll be the happiest man in the world.'

The evening passed so quickly, and they spent most of it sitting together on a sofa and holding hands. Grady seemed grateful for such a peaceful time, and she knew his business gave him little rest. He looked tired as he leaned back and closed his eyes, and Amy ran the tips of her fingers along his strong jawline. He reached up and clutched at her hand.

'Strong and gentle fingers,' he said. 'A doctor's hands. My beloved doctor. Will you nurse me when I'm ill, Amy?'

'Of course,' she replied, smiling. 'But you may not like me in my professional role. I can be stern and unrelenting when I have to. It's a good thing you're taking this holiday next week. You're showing signs of strain and over-work.'

'Yes, Doctor.' He spoke meekly, glancing at her with a glint in his pale eyes. 'It has been a hectic time lately, but those deals had to go through. I needed some extra capital to carry out extensions to the factory. Frank Sandford has put up some of the money, and on the strength of his support I've found aid in London. That was what the trip was all about. That's why I've been playing up to Julia Sandford. She has interests in her father's business, and it was on her agreement that he decided to come in with me.'

'And all your transactions have been completed?' Amy queried.

'Except for signatures on contracts

and things like that. We've reached agreement. That's why I can relax now. I might have to attend some business in London next week, but as we're going up to town for a few days I can kill two birds with one stone.' He sighed. 'In future I'm spending less time at the office. I pay a good staff high wages to take some of the load off my shoulders, and I still do most of the work. I'm going to change all that. A man needs some free time for his family.'

Later he drove her home, and Amy was thoughtful as she took her leave of him. Rain spattered down around her as she watched him drive away, and then she went in tiredly to bed.

The morning seemed to come all too soon, and she was still tired as she prepared to go to the hospital. Aunt Marjorie put a good breakfast in front of her, but Amy did not feel hungry. There was a pang of uneasiness in the back of her mind, and it troubled her. Was it premonition? Everything was going extremely well for her now. There were no clouds gathering on her horizon.

'Is something bothering you, Amy?' her aunt demanded. 'You've hardly eaten a thing this morning.'

'It's nothing, Aunt,' she replied. 'I'm feeling on top of the world, but I'm tired. I've had one or two late nights and I'm not used to that sort of thing.' She smiled as she thought of Grady. 'Perhaps it's the thought of my holiday next week. I'm not used to holidays.'

'I hope you'll have a nice time,' Aunt Marjorie replied. 'It's about time you got away from it all and forgot about Barnbridge and the hospital for a spell.'

'There will be a lot of changes in the future, Aunt,' Amy said wisely.

'I hope they will be good ones,' her aunt told her.

The day at the hospital started like any normal day, and Amy tried to lose herself in the routine to keep the troubled thoughts out of her mind. There was no reason why she should feel uneasy, but the feeling persisted.

Later, when Grady rang, she found worry in his opening words.

'Amy, I'm sorry but I shan't be able to see you this evening,' he greeted her. 'Something has come up. I must see some people.'

'You sound worried, Grady,' she replied. 'Is anything wrong?'

'Nothing more than usual. We do get these alarms in business. Jane wants to know if she'll see you this evening. If you care to come up to the house I'll try and get away as early as I can.'

'All right, Grady. Don't worry about it. Tell Jane she can expect me at about seven. I don't like the idea of her being left to herself. Time is still early, Grady.'

'You're an angel, Doctor Amy,' he said, and the worried tone disappeared from his voice. 'If I don't see you this evening then I'll call you tomorrow. Goodbye.'

After he had hung up Amy sat staring at the wall of her office. She felt that something was wrong, and his voice had betrayed worry. But it had nothing to do with her. It was the pressure of his business, and she hoped that he would be able to handle it.

During the afternoon Tony Walker called her, asking if she were free for the evening.

'I'm sorry, Tony, but I do have to go out this evening. Is there anything special you want to see me about?'

'I just wanted to see you,' he replied. 'But if you'll be busy then forget I called. I can wait.'

'All right. Goodbye, Tony.'

'So long.' The line went dead, and Amy replaced her receiver. She didn't know why she felt sad as the afternoon frittered away.

After duty was over for the day she hurried home, and wasted no time in preparing to go out. Aunt Marjorie made no comment, but insisted that she ate her tea.

'Grady won't be there this evening,' Amy said. 'I'll have to bring Jane around to meet you, Aunt. You'll like her. She's a nice girl. I'm glad we're getting along together.'

'You're satisfied with the way things are going?'

'More than satisfied.' Amy smiled at her aunt. 'Don't look so worried. I'm old enough to know my own mind. I shan't make any mistakes, Aunt.'

'I know you won't dear, but I can't help worrying about you. All the trouble you've had these past three years. I want to see an end to it all. If you got hurt again you'd never get over it.'

'I know, but I have a feeling that everything will be all right. Time will prove me right or wrong.'

She went then to Pent's Hill, eager to see Jane, and when she arrived the child was impatiently waiting. The front door opened before Amy's car drew to a halt outside, and the girl came out to greet her.

'Jane, you shouldn't come out into this keen air with no coat on.'

'Sorry, Doctor Amy, but I've been waiting such a long time to see you. You know that Daddy had to go out, didn't you?'

'Yes, dear, and I came specially to see you. We'll let your Daddy handle his business, but we've got plans to make. It is only a few days now to Monday, and we want to be sure of what we're going to do.'

The child was deliriously happy, and all too soon it was time for her to go to bed. She was reluctant to go, but Amy was insistent, and she cheered up with the reminder that Monday would come all the quicker for an early night. Amy took her up and helped her change. The housekeeper brought some hot milk, and Amy took her leave. She went down to the library and wandered around, looking at the books on the long shelves. She wanted badly to see Grady, but decided against waiting for him to return. He might be very late, and she needed an early night. She let the housekeeper know that she was leaving, and departed.

As she drove home she felt the

uneasiness again in the back of her mind. She didn't like it. In the past three years of loneliness she had developed a sixth sense. Her sensitiveness had intensified, and the feeling that something was wrong kept getting stronger. As she put her car away she tried to fight the feeling off, but it persisted. It had been with her all day, and it wouldn't go now until she went to sleep. Perhaps she was overtired, she thought. Her aunt would be glad to see her in early. She had no wish to cause concern, but she knew that her aunt worried needlessly.

She heard voices in the kitchen when she entered through the front, and frowned, thinking that her uncle was spending one of his rare evenings in. Then she recognised Tony's voice, and hesitated. For some reason she didn't want to talk to him tonight. She felt badly about the way she had been unable to reciprocate his feelings for her. Then she sighed and went into the kitchen.

'Hello,' Tony said, smiling. 'You're in early. I thought you were to be out all evening.'

'I've just been visiting an ex-patient,' she replied. 'It is nice to see you, Tony.'

'I'm glad you're in early, Amy,' Aunt Marjorie told her. 'I was telling Tony just now that you needed a good rest.'

'You'll get that next week, or will you?' he asked, his bright eyes on her face. 'I wish I could take a holiday when I wanted one. Some people have all the luck.'

'I haven't been very lucky yet in my life,' she countered.

'That's true. Don't take any notice of me, Amy. I'm just naturally disgruntled. Come and sit down. I was telling your aunt just now that Barnbridge won't be the same any more. You are dropping out of my life, and we shan't have Julia Sandford around much longer to brighten up the town with her doings.'

'Julia?' Amy was instantly on her guard. 'What's she planning now?' She could remember Julia's words over the telephone. Julia had intended getting Grady for herself. She had even warned Amy to stay away from him. It didn't seem like Julia to get out without a fight. 'Is she leaving Barnbridge?'

'It seems like it. She came into my office this afternoon and instructed me to handle her affairs. She's withdrawing from her father's business and she's going to London. It seems that she doesn't like the simple life any more. She's heading for the bright spots, and she doesn't care who she hurts. Her father rang me after she had left, wanting to know what she was going to do. He's up to his neck in business deals right now and Julia is moving out with half their assets.'

'Frank Sandford has just completed a deal with Grady,' Amy said. She took a quick breath. Was this the reason for her uneasiness of the day? Could this be the trouble she had felt was coming?

'I don't know much about Frank Sandford's business, but if he and Gilmour were relying upon Julia's money to help them then they are doomed to disappointment. Julia is a spiteful female, and there's nothing she wouldn't do to get her own way. You know that she's had her eye on Grady Gilmour for some time, Amy, and from what I know of the situation Gilmour doesn't want to know her. The word has already got around that you and Gilmour are seeing a lot of each other. I think that's what has started Julia off on this wild idea of hers. She'd wreck the whole town to get her own way.'

'Poor Grady.' Amy stared at her aunt. 'He was only saying last night that everything in the garden was lovely.'

'Well it isn't now,' Tony informed her. 'A blight has set in. She's lovely, but no less a blight. But I shouldn't worry about this if I were you, Amy. Gilmour has a good reputation in business, and he should be able to get other backing for what he has in mind. I could never understand in the first place why he went to Sandford, but I suppose he didn't know about Julia then. He's learned his lesson now, I fear, and he should be able to put matters right.'

'I hope so.' Amy shook her head. She knew just how vindictive Julia could be. The girl had told her openly that she intended marrying Grady, and no one in Barnbridge had ever been able to get the better of Julia Sandford. Between the girl and her father lay most of the business interests of the town, and although Frank Sandford held all the power because of his position, he had never been man enough to stand up against his daughter. She always got what she wanted, no matter the man. But that was before she met Grady.

'It's about time Julia Sandford met her match,' Aunt Marjorie said mildly.

'She's had a good innings,' Tony agreed. 'I haven't had much time for Grady Gilmour because you became interested in him, Amy.' He smiled thinly. 'But I believe in giving credit where it is due. He's doing a lot to put Barnbridge on the map, industrially speaking, and he deserves all the help he can get.'

Amy smiled. Grady was a good man. She knew that. It was a pity that someone like Julia could let her business stand or fall with her personal life. But if Grady could get his money elsewhere then he should try. He would never know where he stood with Julia.

'Well I think I'll be going,' Tony said, getting to his feet. 'It's early yet, but you're having an early night, aren't you, Amy?'

'Yes.' She nodded and sighed. 'I'm not used to a hectic pace. I'll wash my hair and then call it a day.'

She went to the door with Tony, and he did not linger, although she had the feeling that he would like to. She felt sorry for him as she closed the door after him. Her own life had changed out of all proportion, but it seemed that trouble was beginning to make itself felt around Grady, and she wondered if it was because she had entered his life. It was a silly thought, but she knew that some people believed in luck to the extent that a few unfortunates could go through life making trouble for everyone they contacted. She hoped that Grady was not superstitious.

Amy washed her hair and took a hot drink to bed with her. She settled in bed with a book, intending to read herself into a sleepy frame of mind, but she could not concentrate upon the printed pages. Her mind kept going off at a tangent, wondering about Grady, hoping that he was able to put his suddenly precarious business state back upon a firm footing. She sighed heavily as she put down the book and turned out the light. She was utterly tired, but sleep would not come. She kept seeing pictures of Julia Sandford's face, and she knew that Julia would make as much trouble as she could for Grady. She was the spiteful kind, and would take malicious pleasure in causing as much harm as she could in the name of thwarted love. A girl like Julia didn't know the real meaning of the word love. That much was obvious, and the sooner Julia herself realized that the better for everyone.

By degrees Amy did fall asleep, and she lay mindless until the sound of the telephone cut through to her inner brain. She came awake instantly, alert and tense, and she heard the phone ringing monotonously. She switched on her bedside lamp and glanced at her watch. A quarter to one! She listened intently, wondering if the call was for her uncle or herself. Then she heard her aunt returning. There was a tap at the door, and Aunt Marjorie peered in.

'Was that call for me, Aunt?'

'Yes, dear. It's Grady Gilmour. He's waiting to talk to you; said it was terribly urgent.'

'Jane,' Amy cried, throwing back the covers and springing out of bed. She reached for her dressing gown and thrust her feet into her slippers. 'It must be Jane. He wouldn't call at this time for anything else.'

'Don't upset yourself, Amy,' her aunt said firmly.

Amy rushed from the room and

hurried down the stairs. The telephone receiver was off the hook, lying on the small table in the hall, and she snatched it up, breathless, fearful and anxious.

'Grady, are you there?' she said urgently. 'This is Amy. What's wrong?' She caught her breath. 'Is it Jane?'

'It is Jane.' Grady's voice was heavy, filled with suppressed emotion. 'Amy, she's not in her room. She's left the house. I think she's run away again.'

'Oh no!' Amy stood frozen for a moment, transfixed with the horror of the picture which came unbidden to her mind; a picture of a small girl running blindly through the night, lost and fearful and hopeless. 'She was all right when I left her earlier, Grady. Are you sure she's not in the house?'

'I've searched it from top to bottom, and the grounds,' came his ragged reply. He was breathing heavily. 'I'm sorry to trouble you at this hour. I suppose I've disturbed the whole household. But I just had to ring you, Amy.'

'You did the right thing, Grady,' she retorted, the shock receding from her mind. 'Have you rung the police and alerted them?'

'Not yet. I'm still shocked by what's happened. 'I could only think of you.'

'Give me fifteen minutes, Grady. I'll get dressed and come up to Pent's Hill immediately.' Amy's training and long experience in emergencies came to her aid. She hung up quickly, turning to find her aunt standing on the bottom stair, and she quickly explained what had happened while she started back up the stairs. Within a few minutes she was hurrying out of the house.

10

Amy drove quickly along the deserted streets, trying to keep her mind in focus. Poor little Jane Gilmour! What had happened to chase her out of that big house again? She set her teeth against the agony and worry that flooded her. The girl had been all right earlier in the evening. What had happened to set her off again?

All the lights were on in the front of the house as Amy drove up the drive. She brought the car to a screeching halt in front of the big door, and sprang out and hurried forward. The door opened before she reached it, and Grady stood there, haggard and utterly exhausted. His eyes were in shadows from the light overhead, but she could see his expression. He was like a man in the last stages of desperation.

'Thank God you're here, Amy!' he rapped.

'Have you found her yet?' she demanded.

He shook his head, his lips thin and uncompromising. He was breathing heavily, and there was anguish on his face.

'What's happened to start this again?' Amy demanded. 'Have you seen her at all this evening, Grady, after you went out earlier?'

'No. I got back here about ten. I'd had a couple of business meetings. I'm in financial trouble at the moment, and I've been trying to find a solution. But that doesn't matter. What happened is this. I'd hardly got in here when I heard a car in the drive outside. I thought it was you, but when I opened the door I found Julia out there. She'd organised the whole damned evening, giving me trouble through her father. She briefed him well enough, and she's put the bar up against me in every other place in Barnbridge. She'd come here to gloat over me. Can you beat that? I'd told her a couple of days ago that there was no future for her in my life. She knew I was in love with you because I told her so. This is her revenge. Hell hath no fury like a woman scorned!' He drew a long breath, shaking his head.

'What happened, Grady?' Amy demanded. 'Time is slipping away. We've got to do something about Jane.'

'Like a fool I let Julia in here for a few minutes. She's like a demented woman when she really lets go of herself. She'd been drinking heavily during the evening, I'd say, and she started shouting. We had a good slanging match in here for a while. I lost my temper because of the way she was using her business interests to get at me. I should have known better. It wasn't until it was too late that I remembered Jane was in the house. I went up to her bedroom and found the room empty. The bed was rumpled, but Jane was gone. I've looked everywhere inside and outside the house. She's not to be found. She must have run away again.'

'Where is Julia now?'

'I sent her packing as soon as I found Jane missing. That poor child! She hasn't been out of hospital two days. I could have throttled Julia! If anything happens to Jane this time I'll make Julia wish she had never been born.'

'You think Jane heard you and Julia shouting, was afraid, and ran off?' Amy demanded. 'I can't believe she would do a thing like that.'

'You don't know the half of it,' Grady said in low, vibrant tones. 'Marion was like that most of the time, shouting and raving about this and that. Many's the time I've had to go up to Jane because the voices awakened her. I think that's what must have happened tonight. She heard us, came to herself, and probably thought the old days had returned. She must have run out of the house in a blind panic. Right now she could be lying out there in the night, dying from exposure.'

'You say you came in about ten. It's one o'clock now. When did Julia arrive?'

'About ten-thirty. I tried to talk some

sense into her before she finally showed her hand. She has no intention of putting any money into my business. She wouldn't marry me now if I was the last man in the world — her words, not mine — and she's going to do everything she can to bring me to my knees.'

'Have you any idea how long Jane has been out of the house?' Amy pursued. 'Do you know where she might make for? How is she dressed? Grady, you've got to pull yourself together. We must find Jane and do it quickly. If she gets a fresh chill after that bout of pneumonia all the drugs in the world won't save her.'

'I don't know what clothes she's got. Her nightdress is upstairs lying on her bed, so she must have dressed in something. I've got no idea where she might go. The last time she wanted to find her mother, but this time — who knows?' He shrugged helplessly. 'What can we do, Amy? If anything happens to her I'll never be able to forgive myself.'

'I'll take a look in her room and see if I can guess what's missing,' Amy said firmly. 'I've got some idea of the clothes she's got. You'd better ring the police and report her missing. They'll get patrols out. She can't have gone far in the night. She may be hiding somewhere in the darkness near the house.'

'They won't be able to find her before daylight,' Grady said hopelessly. 'This cold weather will kill her before then, Amy.'

'Get on the phone,' she rapped, moving to the door. 'I'll look in her room.' She hurried to the stairs, and as she ascended she heard Grady speaking into the telephone.

At the top of the stairs she met the housekeeper.

'Thank God you're here, Doctor!' the woman said, using the time-honoured greeting. 'You must find that poor child before something happens to her.'

'Have you any idea where she might have gone?' Amy queried as they walked into Jane's bedroom.

'No idea at all. I didn't see her after you put her to bed. This is a dreadful business. Mr Gilmour should never had allowed that madwoman in the house.'

'Something will be said to her later, no doubt,' Amy said. 'But the thing to do right now is find Jane. Come and look at her clothes, and perhaps you'll be able to say what's she's wearing.'

'I've already done that. The police will want a description if Mr Gilmour rings them.'

'He's doing that now. Perhaps you'll go down and give him the information.'

Amy went on into the bedroom while the housekeeper went back down the stairs. She stared at the rumpled bed, the discarded nightdress which she had helped Jane into earlier that evening. Had the child left a note? She wandered hopefully around the bedroom, but found nothing. She shook her head disconsolately, wondering about the child. What frame of mind would Jane be in now? Had it happened as Grady imagined? Had the sound of angry voices awakened the child from her sleep, to send her fleeing from the house? Amy sighed heavily and went back down the stairs. She found Grady standing beside the housekeeper, who was giving the police a description of the clothes she thought Jane might be wearing. The woman was shouting into the telephone about a red coat. Amy beckoned Grady to one side.

'I shan't be of any use around here, Grady,' she said. 'I think I'll cruise around the area in my car. I might be lucky and spot her.'

'I shall do that after the police have been,' he said. 'They're sending a car up here, and asked me to wait until they arrive.' He caught at her hands. 'I hope we can find her, Amy.'

'So do I.' Amy pulled herself free and hurried to the door. Her tiredness was gone now, and she went out into the night and climbed into her car. With the headlights full on she drove away and sent the vehicle fast along the winding road. She didn't think Jane would keep to the darker areas. But she didn't know the girl's destination. Pent's Hill was on the edge of town. There had been no sign of Jane on her drive to Pent's Hill, and she thought the girl might keep away from the main roads if she didn't want to be seen. Accordingly, Amy drove to the outskirts and started along the country road.

Her headlamps cut a bright swathe through the darkness, and Amy sat tensed in her seat, her eyes scanning the road ahead. What would a young child alone in the darkness, with her heart filled with trouble, think about? She could not begin to guess at Jane's state of mind. She prayed as she drove that every next moment would bring her sight of the slight figure, but she went on and on without sighting anything. The road was deserted.

When she had covered five miles Amy halted the car and backed into a gateway to turn around. Jane couldn't have covered so much distance. The child must have gone in another direction. Amy knew the area extremely well, and when she came to a side road she took it, knowing that it passed Pent's Hill on it's route to a nearby village. She began to feel hopeful as she followed it. Jane might have left the house and used the back gate to get away. She would have found this road, and even now she might be walking towards the village of Brompton, six miles distant.

Amy sent the car along as fast as she dared, knowing that she would have warning of another vehicle by its lights. She passed Pent's Hill on her right, and continued without slowing, her eyes aching from the strain of staring at the farthermost limits of her lights. Jane, she kept thinking, where are you? Where have you gone? What's in your mind?'

Her tiredness was still in her system, although the urgency of the situation had chased it into her subconscious. Amy dozed over the wheel without being aware of it. She was quickly brought back to full alertness by the glaring light of two headlamps coming towards her. She shook her head and blinked her eyes, dipping her lights as she braked sharply. The other driver sounded the horn, but there was not enough room for them to pass each other. They halted their cars with less than three yards between them.

Amy sat slumped in her seat for a moment. She switched off her headlamps, and wound down her window as a figure appeared at the side of the car. She saw the uniform of a policeman, and took a long breath.

'You were driving recklessly, Madam,' the policeman said thinly. 'What are you doing out at this time of the morning? Would you mind getting out of the car?'

'I haven't been drinking, if that's what you're thinking,' Amy said slowly. 'I was almost asleep though, and perhaps it was a good thing that you came along. I'm Doctor Amy Merrill. I'm looking for a seven-year-old girl who's missing from her home.'

'I see.' There was slightly more animation in the keen tones. 'We've received a call about the child. Where have you searched?'

Amy gave him the details, and explained where she had been making for. She got out of the car to get some fresh air and to stretch her legs, and the policeman called to the driver of the police car to switch off his headlamps.

'We've just come from Brompton,' he said. 'There was no sign of her. We drove out on the main road and came back on this one, intending to go as far as Pent's Hill, but if you've just come from there then there's no sense us covering the same ground. I suppose she would stick to the roads, wouldn't she?'

'I don't know,' Amy replied. 'I think she was suffering from nerves and fright when she left home. She might do anything.'

'It was the same child who ran away from home two or three weeks ago,' the constable said.

'I know,' Amy said tiredly. 'She was in my care at the hospital. She only returned home yesterday.'

'Had pneumonia, didn't she?' The constable shook his head. 'She'll be lucky if she gets off so lightly this time. It's a raw night. We'd better continue with the search, and you'd do well to keep your window open a bit for the fresh air, Doctor. You wouldn't be the first person to drop off to sleep behind the wheel. If you didn't kill yourself you'd probably wake up in your own hospital. Where are you going next?'

'I don't know. Perhaps I'd better return to the house and find out if there's any news.'

'Wait a minute and we'll get through on the radio.' The constable turned to the police car, and Amy heard the sound of voices. She shivered as she stared around into the darkness. Was Jane wandering around somewhere out in this? If the child was still walking then she would already be in trouble. Her lungs would not be able to take the dank night air for long without some adverse effect. She straightened as the constable came back to her. 'There's no report yet of her having been found,' he said in official tones. 'So we'll have to go on with the search.'

'If only we knew where to look,' Amy said. 'I feel so helpless just driving around. She might be huddled asleep in some wet ditch.'

'If she is then likely she'll be dead by morning. If you're going back the way you came, Doctor, then you'd better back up a bit. There's a gateway about twenty yards to your right. Reverse into it and pull out the other way.'

Amy thanked him, and he watched her move the car, using his torch to see that she found the gateway, and she drove off back towards Pent's Hill with his good wishes ringing in her ears.

Her hopelessness was a familiar feeling as she drove back to Grady's home. She had lived with it for more than three years. It had fled with the onset of love for Grady and Jane, but it had not departed from her system. It had lain in wait in the darker recesses of her mind, ready to take over again should disaster strike. She shook her head, a picture of Jane's face showing on the broad stretch of her imagination. The girl had been so happy the evening before. All her difficulties had smoothed away. Now she was wandering around in the night, barely recovered from pneumonia, and Amy shuddered to think of the damage that was being done to the youngster by the cold night air.

She had to drive by a circuitous route to reach the front of Grady's house, and as she went up the drive towards the big lighted building she prayed that a miracle had happened, that Jane had returned to the warmth and security of her bed.

Grady came to the door as her car stopped. Amy could see horror on his face. He stared hopefully at her, looking in the car for sign of his daughter, and Amy's hopes fled in unison with his. She was expecting to hear that the child had come home and he wanted to see her in the car.

'I've searched everywhere in the neighbourhood, Grady. I couldn't see her. I don't think she walked far. She's not on any of the roads. I expect she's dropped down into some spot and she's lying there waiting for daylight.'

'Then she'll never see it,' he said, taking her arm and leading her into the house. 'This weather will kill her, Amy.' He closed the door on the rawness and took her into the library. 'I feel so damned helpless. The police told me to remain here in case she returned.'

'Well it's no use trying to search for her until daybreak,' Amy told him. 'If you missed her as soon as she had gone there would have been a good chance of spotting her, but she had time to get under cover. She may not be far from the house. Have you got sheds and stables on the premises? Have you searched everywhere in the grounds where she might be hiding?'

'I've looked in every conceivable

place,' he said wearily. 'Would you like a drink? You look half frozen, and I'm sure you must be exhausted.'

'No thank you.' She shook her head. 'Where was she found the last time?'

'You think she might have gone in the same direction?' He found sudden hope. His eyes blazed, then lost their fire. 'She was huddled under a haystack. She caught pneumonia from that. This time it will kill her.'

'Where is the haystack? I'd better go check.'

'I'll come with you,' he said. 'This waiting around is killing me. I'll tell Edith that I'm going out for a bit. She'll be on hand if the police ring or Jane comes back.'

Amy went out to her car and climbed behind the wheel. She wiped the windows and started the engine, shivering as the warm air from the heater touched her clammy skin. Grady came out of the house and climbed in beside her.

'It's a forlorn hope,' he said, 'but we

can't afford to overlook any possibility.'

Amy drove away, and with Grady giving her directions she pushed the car along. They left town by another road, and had covered two miles before Grady leaned forward to peer through the windscreen.

'The haystack should be on the left along here somewhere.'

Amy slowed the car, and they both studied the shadows as they passed. Then Grady uttered an exclamation and pointed at a dark mass which they had passed. Amy pulled on to the verge and they got out of the car. She took her powerful torch from the glove compartment and they walked together through the wide gateway and into the field. Hope filtered through the both of them as they walked forward, but a swift search proved that Jane had not returned to her first hiding place.

'Where ever can she be?' Grady said in agonised tones as they walked back to the car.

'I wish I knew, Grady. I'd give my

right arm to find her now.' Amy sighed. 'We'd better go back to the house. We're not doing any good out here. We'll have to start searching on foot as soon as it gets light.'

As they reached the car they were bathed in the glare of headlamps, and a car drew in behind them. Grady turned, and Amy saw the police sign on the front of the vehicle. A policeman came towards them, and Amy listened to Grady talking to him. She was beginning to feel too tired for speech, and hopelessness had added its dull pangs to her feelings. Each fleeting hour added to the missing child's exposure to the night. If she wasn't soon found then she would die. She shook her head, dragging herself from her thoughts, and listened to Grady talking to the policeman.

'I'm sorry, Mr Gilmour, but there's still no sign of her. Our patrols have covered every yard of the roads. It's obvious that she's found some spot to curl up in. That's why we're here. We suddenly thought that she might have returned to this spot.'

'She's not here,' Grady replied in lifeless tones. 'We've just looked.'

'Then I suggest you return to your house and try to get some rest.' The policeman spoke in kindly tones. 'You'll be wanting to take part in the search tomorrow, and if you don't rest up you won't be able to do what you want.'

'You think I could go back home and rest while my child is dying of exposure out here somewhere?' Grady shook his head. 'I'll keep looking for her. I'll never be able to sleep again if we don't find her in time to save her.'

'Then I suggest you come with us, sir. We have a radio, and we'll be informed the minute there's any news. She could be picked up at any moment, and you would be searching for the rest of the night without knowing.'

'That's a good idea.' Grady turned to Amy. 'I think you should go home now,' he said. 'You've done all you can, Amy, and you have to go to the hospital in the morning.'

'Do you think I shall be able to sleep?' she demanded.

He took her hands. 'I know how you feel,' he said softly. 'But there's nothing can be done until morning. The police are covering every road in the area. Go home, Amy, and get to bed.'

'All right.' She nodded tiredly. 'I'm ready to drop as it is. It will be good sense to call it off for now. I'll check with you in the morning, Grady.'

He nodded, kissed her lightly on the lips, and followed the policeman to the car. Amy watched them drive away, then she sighed and got into her driving seat. For a moment she sat thinking about the situation, but no amount of thought could solve his problem. Jane was gone, and they needed daylight to aid their search.

She slumped a little in her seat as she drove home. Tiredness was like a disease in her brain. She tried to make as little noise as possible when she reached the house. Her uncle would be asleep, but she expected her aunt to

237

be awake and worried. She put the car away and tiptoed towards the house. The door was unlocked, and she entered softly and stood for a moment in the darkness. Then she started for her room. She didn't need a light to guide her, and she was too tired to bother about anything but the warmth and comfort of her bed. She undressed in the dark, dropping her clothes where she stood, and then she tumbled into bed. Despite the worry in her mind she fell asleep immediately, utterly exhausted both mentally and physically, and she lay dreamless until her aunt tapped on her door next morning.

11

Amy awoke with a start, and had to force her eyes open. She sat up in the bed and stared around. Her head was aching dully and she felt dreadful. Something had awakened her, and she wondered what it was. Then she heard the tapping on the door again.

'Come in, Aunt,' she called.

The door opened and Aunt Marjorie entered. She stared at her niece, seeing the strain and the tiredness in her haggard face.

'So they haven't found her yet!'

'Not up to the time I came home.' Amy wearily threw aside the covers. She looked at her clothes strewn on the floor, and picked them up. 'There's been no telephone call, has there?' she demanded.

'No. I'm sorry but there hasn't.'

'That means she's still missing.' Amy

tightened her lips. 'I'd better ring Grady. He must be beside himself with worry.'

'I feel sorry for the child,' Aunt Marjorie said, turning to depart. 'I'll have your breakfast ready when you come down, Amy.'

Amy dressed. She went to the bathroom and bathed her aching eyes. She felt as if she hadn't slept a wink in a month, and could guess how Grady must be feeling. She went down to the kitchen, and Aunt Marjorie poured hot tea for her.

'If that child has been out in the open all night then you won't be able to save her, Amy.'

'I know, Aunt. That's been worrying me ever since I knew she'd gone again.'

'What happened to set her off this time?'

Amy told her aunt, and the older woman suppressed a sigh. Amy sat down to a breakfast she didn't want, but she ate, knowing that she had a full day's work ahead of her at the hospital. When she had finished she went out to the hall to call Grady. She listened to the ringing tone, feeling hopeless, knowing that Grady would have called her if Jane had been found. The housekeeper answered the phone, and told Amy that Grady had been out all night and had not returned. Amy thanked her and hung up. She stood for a moment, all hope gone from her. She knew without doubt that exposure would kill Jane if the child had been out in the open all night.

She turned slowly to go back to the kitchen, and heard the click of the sitting room door opening. Amy turned quickly, thinking it was her uncle, and she saw the door opening slowly.

'Is that you, Uncle?' she called, and went forward, frowning.

The door opened and Amy halted in her tracks. It wasn't her uncle emerging. She stared in disbelief at the small figure, then went running forward to drop to her knees beside the child.

'Jane, where have you come from?' she demanded, taking the girl into her arms. Her eyes burned with tears, and she hugged the child, swamped with relief. Jane put her arms tightly around Amy's neck, clinging as if she would never let go.

'I hope you won't be angry, Doctor Amy. I came here last night to see you. But it was dark, and I didn't want to wake you. The door was undone so I came in and sat in there, on the sofa. I must have fallen asleep. I woke up just now when I heard your voice.'

Amy got to her feet, calling to her aunt, and she studied the girl's face. Jane seemed none the worse for her adventure. She held the girl's hand tightly, turning to face the kitchen as Aunt Marjorie appeared in the doorway.

'This is Jane Gilmour, Aunt,' she said softly. 'She came here last night and spent it in your sitting room.'

'Hello, Jane,' Aunt Marjorie said. 'I expect you're hungry now, aren't you? Come along into the kitchen and I'll give you some breakfast. Doctor Amy has told me such a lot about you, and I've been hoping she would bring you around to see me.'

'I came on my own,' the child said. 'There was a lot of shouting at home. I was frightened when it woke me up. Mummy used to shout at Daddy like that, so I thought I'd come to Doctor Amy.'

The girl went to Aunt Marjorie and took her hand, and as the older woman led the child into the kitchen she glanced over her shoulder at Amy, then motioned to the telephone. Amy nodded, almost overcome now. Relief was stabbing through her, filling her throat with an ache and her eyes with tears. She hurriedly rang the police and passed on the good news, then called Grady's house to tell the housekeeper. As she hung up the receiver she burst into tears, and hurried up to her room and threw herself upon the bed and sobbed. Reaction hit her hard, and then she recovered her composure and went along to the bathroom to repair the ravages of her tears.

She paused outside the kitchen door, listening to Jane's voice as the child spoke to Aunt Marjorie. She heaved a great shuddering sigh of relief, forced a smile to her quivering lips, and went in.

Jane sat at the table, completely at home, and the child smiled at Amy, who sat down at her side.

'Are you angry with me, Doctor Amy, for coming to see you? You've been so good to me that I didn't want to see anyone else.'

'I'm not angry, Jane,' Amy told her thankfully. 'But it was wrong of you to leave the house as you did, without telling anyone where you were going. Your father has been out all night looking for you. After your illness we were afraid that the night air would harm you.'

'I came straight here,' the child said. 'I was afraid to tell Daddy because of the shouting. I knew you would take care of me.'

'I thought you had run away again, Jane.'

'I wouldn't do that!' the girl declared. 'We're going on a holiday next week. I wouldn't ever run away from you, Doctor Amy.'

Amy glanced at the clock. She caught her aunt's eye. The relief inside her was overwhelming. She thought of Grady and knew how he would feel when he heard the news. He would come around immediately, and she wanted to be here to greet him. Aunt Marjorie was smiling, and perhaps sight of her niece's happiness with this child showed her that there was nothing for her to worry about.

The telephone rang, and Amy hurried to answer it. She heard Grady's voice at the other end, and he was choked with emotion. She told him what had happened, and heard his sigh of relief.

'Shall I come for her?' he demanded. 'I shan't go into the office today. I'm worn out. I've been looking around the countryside all night.'

'Perhaps you'd better leave her here for today, Grady,' Amy replied. 'I think Aunt Marjorie will take care of her.

Then I'll bring her home this evening when I get through at the hospital. I should be able to get away early today. It's Saturday.'

'Is it?' He laughed. 'I wouldn't know. I think I'll go to bed for the day. I'll be waiting for you this evening, Amy.'

'There's one thing, Grady,' she said.

'What's that, my beloved doctor?'

'Don't say anything to Jane about this business when she comes home. Let her forget it. This is just a normal visit to my home.'

'If you say so.' He chuckled. 'Thank God the nightmare is over.'

'I know exactly how you feel,' she told him. 'Get some sleep, Grady. Don't forget that next week will be hectic.'

'It can't come quickly enough for me,' he retorted.

Amy hung up and went back to the kitchen.

'That was your father on the telephone,' she said.

'Was he angry with me?' the girl demanded.

'No. He's very happy that you're quite safe and well. He said you did a silly thing by leaving the house as you did, but he forgives you.'

'Is he coming for me? I don't want to go home without you.'

'No, he's not coming. I told him that you would be staying here for the day, if Aunt Marjorie doesn't mind. Then I'll take you home this evening. There's only one more day after this before our holiday starts.'

'Will you stay here with me today?' Aunt Marjorie asked.

'Yes, if you want me.' There was a world of experience in the young voice.

'You'll always be welcome here, Jane.'

Amy went off to the hospital with a light heart. She felt tired but happy, and the day couldn't end quickly enough for her. The tension of the night before was gone, and for the first time in years she felt completely happy. The routine of the day was as nothing. She felt as if she had been granted a new lease of life.

She was finished by three, and took

her leave, hurrying home to Jane. Aunt Marjorie was in the big back garden with the child, and Jane came running to Amy with arms outstretched. Amy closed her eyes as they embraced, and Aunt Marjorie went into the house to leave them to themselves.

'Did my Daddy telephone you at the hospital?' Jane asked.

'No. I told him we'd see him this evening. He said he would sleep because he was awake all last night.'

'I'm sorry if I caused any trouble. At the time it seemed the best thing to do.'

Amy ruffled the child's hair. 'Don't worry about it, Jane. Come along, let's smarten you up and go home. I expect your Daddy is awake now, and he'll be anxious to see you.'

They drove up to the big house on Pent's Hill in the last of the afternoon sunshine. Leaves were falling from the branches overhanging the drive, and as they pulled up in front of the door Grady opened it and came outside. Jane sprang out of the car and ran to him, hurling herself into his waiting arms, and Amy sat for a moment, watching them. Grady peered at her across Jane's shoulder, and his face was showing his complete happiness. He put the girl down and whispered in her ear, and Jane turned to fling a quick, happy glance at Amy before running into the house.

Grady came towards the car as Amy alighted, and there was an intent expression on his strong features. Amy felt a surging rush of emotion as he held his arms out to her, and she hurried to him in much the same way that Jane had done.

His strong arms closed about her in a crushing embrace, and Amy's heart felt so full. His cheek touched hers, and she heard his soft voice.

'Amy, I love you. Will you marry me?'

'Grady,' she whispered. 'What a beautiful question! I don't have to wait any longer to give you my answer. I want you for my husband and Jane for my little girl. I'll marry you.'

He eased back from her, staring into her face, looking into her eyes for some sign that would tell him beyond her words that she would be his, and he found what he was looking for. He smiled slowly, and then kissed her, holding her close in his comforting arms. Amy surrendered to him, and the last vestige of the haunting past in her mind was finally eradicated. She kissed him unashamedly, all defences gone.

'I love you, Grady,' she said when she could get her breath. 'I was afraid at first that I might be disloyal to the memories. But you don't think I am?'

'Not disloyal, Amy, dearest, my beloved doctor! We have both suffered loss, although yours was far greater than mine. You have a right to some happiness, and I think I can give it to you. Don't cry, my love. You've shed more than your share of tears in the past.'

'I'm crying because I am so happy,' she whispered. 'You wouldn't want to stop me, would you?'

'Not for that reason, Amy.' He smiled

tenderly. 'You can cry for the rest of your life so long as you keep the same reason for your tears.'

He swept her back into his arms, and she clung to his neck. As he kissed her again she could hear Jane's happy voice singing somewhere in the house, and her heart seemed to lift with joy. The future was suddenly filled with golden possibility, and she knew the dark days were over.

As Grady turned and led her into the house her mind was already making plans for the future . . .

We do hope that you have enjoyed reading this large print book.

Did you know that all of our titles are available for purchase?

We publish a wide range of high quality large print books including:
Romances, Mysteries, Classics
General Fiction
Non Fiction and Westerns

Special interest titles available in large print are:
The Little Oxford Dictionary
Music Book, Song Book
Hymn Book, Service Book

Also available from us courtesy of Oxford University Press:
Young Readers' Dictionary
(large print edition)
Young Readers' Thesaurus
(large print edition)

For further information or a free brochure, please contact us at:
Ulverscroft Large Print Books Ltd.,
The Green, Bradgate Road, Anstey,
Leicester, LE7 7FU, England.
Tel: (00 44) **0116 236 4325**
Fax: (00 44) **0116 234 0205**

LOVE WILL FIND A WAY

Miranda Barnes

Convalescing after a car accident, Gwen Yorke leases a remote cottage on the beautiful Isle of Skye. She hopes to find inspiration there for her career as a rug designer, and wants to decide if she and her boyfriend have a future together. In Glenbrittle, she finds herself drawn to the enigmatic, moody Andrew McIver, and his young daughter Fiona. To Gwen's delight, she and Fiona become close, frequently sketching together. But why is Andrew so unhappy about their friendship?

THE PRINCE'S BRIDE

Sophie Weston

One of three royal brothers in the Adriatic principality of San Michele, Prince Jonas works hard. But after a protocol-ridden evening, he's due some downtime in his beloved forest. Hope Kennard was the daughter of the manor back in England. But she has guarded her heart since her childhood ended in financial scandal. She's just passing through San Michele, before moving on to another country, another job. But then a charming forest ranger appears. And this time, her instincts don't help . . .

THE UNEXPECTED GIFT

Sarah Purdue

When London nurse Megan Falstaff is informed she's received an inheritance from her beloved godmother Cathleen, she's expecting a couple of cat figurines. What she actually inherits is a boarding cattery in the village of Little River — with the stipulation that she must run it for at least a year. Getting to grips with the eccentricities of felines and village folk alike is challenging for Megan — and matters aren't helped by the disdain of the haughty vet Doctor William Wakefield . . .

ONLY TRUE IN FAIRY TALES

Christine Stovell

Eloise Blake has been fascinated by Prospect House, the shadowy romantic Gothic edifice opposite hers, ever since she moved to the village of Hookfield. When its new owner turns out to be bestselling crime author Ross Farrell, whose work is grounded in gritty reality rather than happy endings, she is determined to concentrate on her tapestry design business and her rescue dog Gracie. Love, she thinks, is only true in fairy tales. But is Ross the Prince Charming she thought didn't exist — or is he a beast in disguise?

THE MAGIC CHARM

Christina Green

When Goldie Smith spies the portrait of the three Crosby girls for the first time, belonging to her dear Great-aunt Mary and painted long ago by an enigmatic local artist, she can't help but wonder at the history behind it. She also takes an instant shine to Rob Tyson, the handsome man who comes to photograph the painting. But his first love seems to be the rare birds he makes extensive trips to record with his camera. Is there room for Goldie in his life as well?

YOU'RE THE ONE
THAT I WANT

Angela Britnell

When Sarah, a teacher from Cornwall, and Matt, a businessman from Nashville, meet on a European coach tour, they soon find themselves in a relationship — a fake one. Because Matt is too bust for romance, and Sarah is only trying to make her ex-husband jealous. For every picturesque destination, there's a loved-up selfie and Facebook post to match. But as their holiday comes to an end, Sarah and Matt realise they're not happy with their pretend relationship. They want the real thing . . .